Gems of Quotations

AN AUTHOR-WISE REFERENCE BOOK

Madhu Sharma

NEW DELHI (INDIA)

Gems of Quotations

Published by

MG BOOKS

An Imprint of

MAANU GRAPHICS

MAANU GRAPHICS

(PUBLISHERS OF GENERAL BOOKS)

5FF, Ganpati Bhawan, 21 Ansari Road,
Darya Ganj, New Delhi-110002
Ph: 65285220, 64138266
E-mail : maanugraphics@yahoo.com
mgbooks.maanu@yahoo.com

Printed at
Satyam Enterprises, Delhi

CONTENTS

A

Adams, John

- But a Constitution of Government once changed from Freedom, can never be restored. Liberty, once lost, is lost forever.
- Children should be educated and instructed in the principles of freedom.
- I always consider the settlement of America with reverence and wonder, as the opening of a grand scene and design in providence, for the illumination of the ignorant and the emancipation of the slavish part of mankind all over the earth.
- I must study politics and war that my sons may have liberty to study mathematics and philosophy. My sons ought to study mathematics and philosophy, geography, natural history, naval architecture, navigation, commerce, and agriculture, in order to give their children a right to study painting, poetry, music, architecture, statuary, tapestry, and porcelain.
- In my many years I have come to a conclusion that one useless man is a shame, two is a law firm, and three or more is a congress.

- No man who ever held the office of president would congratulate a friend on obtaining it.
- The proposition that the people are the best keepers of their own liberties is not true. They are the worst conceivable, they are no keepers at all; they can neither judge, act, think, or will, as a political body.
- We have no government armed with power capable of contending with human passions unbridled by morality and religion. Avarice, ambition, revenge or gallantry would break the strongest cords of our Constitution as a whale goes through a net. Our Constitution is designed only for a moral and religious people. It is wholly inadequate for any other.
- Facts are stubborn things; and whatever may be our wishes, our inclinations, or the dictates of our passion, they cannot alter the state of facts and evidence.
- You will never be alone with a poet in your pocket.
- There is danger from all men. The only maxim of a free government ought to be to trust no man living with power to endanger the public liberty.
- Our obligations to our country never cease but with our lives.
- Democracy never lasts long. It soon wastes, exhausts and murders itself. There was never a democracy that did not commit suicide.

Aesop

- Better be wise by the misfortunes of others than by your own.
- In critical moments even the very powerful have need of the weakest.
- Injuries may be forgiven, but not forgotten.
- It is easy to be brave from a safe distance.
- It is with our passions, as it is with fire and water, they are good servants but bad masters.
- Persuasion is often more effectual than force.
- The smaller the mind the greater the conceit.
- United we stand, divided we fall.
- We hang the petty thieves and appoint the great ones to public office.
- What a splendid head, yet no brain.
- Put your shoulder to the wheel.
- The gods help them that help themselves.
- Be content with your lot; one cannot be first in everything.
- It is thrifty to prepare today for the wants of tomorrow.
- Union gives strength.

- Beware lest you lose the substance by grasping at the shadow.
- People often grudge others what they cannot enjoy themselves.
- The shaft of the arrow had been feathered with one of the eagle's own plumes. We often give our enemies the means of our own destruction.
- I am sure the grapes are sour.
- Familiarity breed contempt.
- Self-conceit may lead to self-destruction.
- Thinking to get at once all the gold the goose could give, he killed it and opened it only to find - nothing.

Alcott, Amos Bronson

- Devotees of grammatical studies have not been distinguished for any very remarkable felicities of expression.
- The true teacher defends his pupils against his own personal influence.
- One must be a wise reader to quote wisely and well.
- Civilization degrades the many to exalt the few.

Allen, Fred

- A celebrity is a person who works hard all his life to become well known, then wears dark glasses to avoid being recognized.
- A conference is a gathering of important people who singly can do nothing, but together can decide that nothing can be done.
- California is a fine place to live—if you happen to be an orange.
- Committee—a group of men who individually can do nothing but as a group decide that nothing can be done.
- Hanging is too good for a man who makes puns; he should be drawn and quoted.
- Hollywood is a place where people from Iowa mistake each other for stars.
- I can't understand why a person will take a year to write a novel when he can easily buy one for a few dollars.
- Imitation is the sincerest form of television.
- What's on your mind, if you will allow the overstatement?
- You can take all the sincerity in Hollywood, place

it in the navel of a firefly and still have room enough for three caraway seeds and a producer's heart.

- Television is a new medium. It's called a medium because nothing is well-done.

Allen, Woody

- As the poet said, 'Only God can make a tree' — probably because it's so hard to figure out how to get the bark on.
- Eighty percent of success is showing up.
- Eternal nothingness is fine if you happen to be dressed for it.
- His lack of education is more than compensated for by his keenly developed moral bankruptcy.
- How can I believe in God when just last week I got my tongue caught in the roller of an electric typewriter?
- How is it possible to find meaning in a finite world, given my waist and shirt size?
- I am at two with nature.
- I can't listen to that much Wagner. I start getting the urge to conquer Poland.
- I don't want to achieve immortality through my

work... I want to achieve it through not dying.

- I took a speed reading course and read 'War and Peace' in twenty minutes. It involves Russia.
- I was thrown out of college for cheating on the metaphysics exam; I looked into the soul of the boy sitting next to me.
- I'm astounded by people who want to 'know' the universe when it's hard enough to find your way around Chinatown.
- If it turns out that there is a God, I don't think that he's evil. But the worst that you can say about him is that basically he's an underachiever.
- If only God would give me some clear sign! Like making a large deposit in my name in a Swiss bank.
- Interestingly, according to modern astronomers, space is finite. This is a very comforting thought—particularly for people who can never remember where they have left things.
- It is impossible to experience one's death objectively and still carry a tune.
- It is impossible to travel faster than the speed of light, and certainly not desirable, as one's hat keeps blowing off.
- It seemed the world was divided into good and

bad people. The good ones slept better... while the bad ones seemed to enjoy the waking hours much more.

- Life is divided into the horrible and the miserable.
- Life is full of misery, loneliness, and suffering - and it's all over much too soon.
- Money is better than poverty, if only for financial reasons.
- Most of the time I don't have much fun. The rest of the time I don't have any fun at all.
- My education was dismal. I went to a series of schools for mentally disturbed teachers.
- My one regret in life is that I am not someone else.
- Not only is there no God, but try getting a plumber on weekends.
- On the plus side, death is one of the few things that can be done just as easily lying down.
- Organized crime in America takes in over forty billion dollars a year and spends very little on office supplies.
- Students achieving Oneness will move on to Twoness.
- The government is unresponsive to the needs of the little man. Under 5'7", it is impossible to get your congressman on the phone.

Aristotle

- A flatterer is a friend who is your inferior, or pretends to be so.
- A friend is a second self.
- All human actions have one or more of these seven causes: chance, nature, compulsion, habit, reason, passion, and desire.
- All paid jobs absorb and degrade the mind.
- All virtue is summed up in dealing justly.
- Dignity consists not in possessing honors, but in the consciousness that we deserve them.
- Education is the best provision for the journey to old age.
- Happiness depends upon ourselves.
- Humor is the only test of gravity, and gravity of humor; for a subject which will not bear raillery is suspicious, and a jest which will not bear serious examination is false wit.
- It is in justice that the ordering of society is centered.
- It is the mark of an educated mind to be able to entertain a thought without accepting it.
- It is unbecoming for young men to utter maxims.

- Law is mind without reason.
- Man perfected by society is the best of all animals; he is the most terrible of all when he lives without law, and without justice.
- Men acquire a particular quality by constantly acting a particular way... you become just by performing just actions, temperate by performing temperate actions, brave by performing brave actions.
- One swallow does not make a summer, neither does one fine day; similarly one day or brief time of happiness does not make a person entirely happy.
- Pleasure in the job puts perfection in the work.
- Poverty is the parent of revolution and crime.
- The gods too are fond of a joke.
- The moral virtues, then, are produced in us neither by nature nor against nature. Nature, indeed, prepares in us the ground for their reception, but their complete formation is the product of habit.
- The only stable state is the one in which all men are equal before the law.
- To give a satisfactory decision as to the truth it is necessary to be rather an arbitrator than a party to the dispute.
- To perceive is to suffer.

- We are what we repeatedly do.
- Young people are in a condition like permanent intoxication, because youth is sweet and they are growing.
- It is not always the same thing to be a good man and a good citizen.
- Evil brings men together.
- Misfortune shows those who are not really friends.
- Wretched, ephemeral race, children of chance and tribulation, why do you force me to tell you the very thing which it would be most profitable for you not to hear? The very best thing is utterly beyond your reach: not to have been born, not to be, to be nothing. However, the second best thing for you is: to die soon.

Armstrong, Louis

- What we play is life.
- Making money ain't nothing exciting to me. You might be able to buy a little better booze than the wino on the corner. But you get sick just like the next cat and when you die you're just as graveyard dead as he is.

Arnold, Matthew

- The freethinking of one age is the common sense of the next.
- The true meaning of religion is thus not simply morality, but morality touched by emotion.
- Resolve to be thyself: and know, that he who finds himself, loses his misery.
- Truth sits upon the lips of dying men.

Auden, W. H.

- Among those whom I like or admire, I can find no common denominator, but among those whom I love, I can: all of them make me laugh.
- Evil is unspectacular and always human, And shares our bed and eats at our own table.
- False enchantment can last a lifetime.
- Murder is unique in that it abolishes the party it injures, so that society has to take the place of the victim and on his behalf demand atonement or grant forgiveness; it is the one crime in which society has a direct interest.
- No opera plot can be sensible, for people do not sing when they are feeling sensible.

- One cannot review a bad book without showing off.
- Some books are undeservedly forgotten; none are undeservedly remembered.
- We are here on Earth to do good to others. What the others are here for, I don't know.
- A poet's hope: to be, like some valley cheese, local, but prized elsewhere.

Austen, Jane

- I do not want people to be agreeable, as it saves me the trouble of liking them.
- To sit in the shade on a fine day, and look upon verdure is the most perfect refreshment.
- Where so many hours have been spent in convincing myself that I am right, is there not some reason to fear I may be wrong?
- One half of the world cannot understand the pleasures of the other.
- Silly things do cease to be silly if they are done by sensible people in an impudent way.
- A large income is the best recipe for happiness I ever heard of.

- Everybody likes to go their own way—to choose their own time and manner of devotion.
- I cannot think well of a man who sports with any woman's feelings; and there may often be a great deal more suffered than a stander-by can judge of.
- I pay very little regard...to what any young person says on the subject of marriage. If they profess a disinclination for it, I only set it down that they have not yet seen the right person.
- If any one faculty of our nature may be called more wonderful than the rest, I do think it is memory. There seems something more speakingly incomprehensible in the powers, the failures, the inequalities of memory, than in any other of our intelligences. The memory is sometimes so retentive, so serviceable, so obedient; at others, so bewildered and so weak; and at others again, so tyrannic, so beyond control! We are, to be sure, a miracle every way; but our powers of recollecting and of forgetting do seem peculiarly past finding out.
- It will, I believe, be everywhere found, that as the clergy are, or are not what they ought to be, so are the rest of the nation.
- Nothing amuses me more than the easy manner with which everybody settles the abundance of those who have a great deal less than themselves.
- Oh! Do not attack me with your watch. A watch is always too fast or too slow. I cannot be dictated

to by a watch.

- One cannot fix one's eyes on the commonest natural production without finding food for a rambling fancy.
- The enthusiasm of a woman's love is even beyond the biographer's.
- There will be little rubs and disappointments everywhere, and we are all apt to expect too much; but then, if one scheme of happiness fails, human nature turns to another; if the first calculation is wrong, we make a second better: we find comfort somewhere.
- We have all a better guide in ourselves, if we would attend to it, than any other person can be.
- Where any one body of educated men, of whatever denomination, are condemned indiscriminately, there must be a deficiency of information, or...of something else.
- But when a young lady is to be a heroine, the perverseness of forty surrounding families cannot prevent her. Something must and will happen to throw a hero in her way.
- Friendship is certainly the finest balm for the pangs of disappointed love.
- In every power, of which taste is the foundation,

excellence is pretty fairly divided between the sexes.

- It is a truth universally acknowledged, that a single man in possession of a good fortune, must be in want of a wife.

B

Bacon, Sir Francis

- A wise man will make more opportunities than he finds.
- By far the best proof is experience.
- Certainly virtue is like precious odors, most fragrant when they are incensed, or crushed: for prosperity doth best discover vice, but adversity doth best discover virtue.
- Choose the life that is most useful, and habit will make it the most agreeable.
- Death is a friend of ours; and he that is not ready to entertain him is not at home.
- Discretion in speech is more than eloquence.
- He of whom many are afraid ought to fear many.
- Hope is a good breakfast, but it is a bad supper.
- I have taken all knowledge to be my province.
- If a man will begin with certainties, he shall end in doubts; but if he will be content to begin with doubts he shall end in certainties.

- In taking revenge, a man is but even with his enemy; but in passing it over, he is superior.
- Natural abilities are like natural plants; they need pruning by study.
- Praise from the common people is generally false, and rather follows the vain than the virtuous.
- Read not to contradict and confute, nor to find talk and discourse, but to weigh and consider.
- Read not to contradict and confute, not to believe and take for granted, not to find talk and discourse, but to weigh and consider.
- Reading maketh a full man, conference a ready man, and writing an exact man.
- Revenge is a kind of wild justice, which the more man's nature runs to the more ought law to weed it out.
- Seek ye first the good things of the mind, and the rest will either be supplied or its loss will not be felt.
- Silence is the virtue of fools.
- Some books are to be tasted, others to be swallowed, and some few to be chewed and digested: that is, some books are to be read only in parts, others to be read, but not curiously, and some few to be read wholly, and with diligence and attention.

- The worst solitude is to be destitute of sincere friendship.
- They are ill discoverers that think there is no land, when they can see nothing but sea.
- There is no excellent beauty that hath not some strangeness in the proportion.
- Men fear death as children fear to go in the dark; and as that natural fear in children is increased by tales, so is the other.
- Houses are built to live in, not to look on; therefore, let use be preferred before uniformity, except where both may be had.
- Knowledge is power.

Bagehot, Walter

- One of the greatest pains to human nature is the pain of a new idea.
- The greatest mistake is trying to be more agreeable than you can be.
- The greatest pleasure in life is doing what people say you cannot do.
- The habit of common and continuous speech is a symptom of mental deficiency.

- The reason why so few good books are written is that so few people who can write know anything.
- The whole history of civilization is strewn with creeds and institutions which were invaluable at first, and deadly afterwards.
- It is good to be without vices, but it is not good to be without temptations.

Bakunin, Mikhail

- The freedom of all is essential to my freedom.
- I reverse the phrase of Voltaire, and say that if God really existed, it would be necessary to abolish him.

Barrie, James M.

- A safe but sometimes chilly way of recalling the past is to force open a crammed drawer. If you are searching for anything in particular you don't find it, but something falls out at the back that is often more interesting.
- Always be a little kinder than necessary.
- Ambition - it is the last infirmity of noble minds.
- Dreams do come true, if we only wish hard enough, You can have anything in life if you will sacrifice everything else for it.

- Everytime a child says 'I don't believe in fairies' there is a little fairy somewhere that falls down dead.
- For several days after my first book was published, I carried it about in my pocket and took surreptitious peeps at it to make sure the ink had not faded.
- His lordship may compel us to be equal upstairs, but there will never be equality in the servants hall.
- I know not, sir, whether Bacon wrote the works of Shakespeare, but if he did not it seems to me that he missed the opportunity of his life.
- I'm youth, I'm joy, I'm a little bird that has broken out of the egg.
- If you have love you don't need to have anything else. If you don't have it it doesn't matter much what else you do have.
- Let no one who loves be unhappy, even love unreturned has its rainbow.
- Life is a long lesson in humility.
- Never ascribe to an opponent motives meaner than your own.
- Nothing is really work unless you would rather be doing something else.
- Strength instead of being the lusty child of passions, grows by grappling with and subduing them.

- Temper is a weapon that we hold by the blade.
- That is ever the way. 'Tis all jealousy to the bride and good wishes to the corpse.
- The best place a person can die, is where they die for others.
- The life of every man is a diary in which he means to write one story, and writes another; and his humblest hour is when he compares the volume as it is with what he vowed to make it.
- The most useless are those who never change through the years.
- The praise that comes from love does not make us vain, but more humble.
- The secret of happiness in not in what one likes to do, but in what one has to do.
- There are few more impressive sights in the world than a Scotsman on the make.
- Those who bring sunshine into the lives of others cannot keep it from themselves.
- To die will be an awfully big adventure.
- We are all of us failures, at least, the best of us are.
- We never understand how little we need in this world until we know the loss of it.
- You must have been warned against letting the golden hours slip by; but some of them are golden only because we let them slip by.

- God gave us memory so that we might have roses in December.

Barrymore, John

- America is the country where you buy a lifetime supply of aspirin for one dollar and use it up in two weeks.
- Happiness often sneaks in through a door you didn't know you left open.
- Love is the delightful interval between meeting a beautiful girl and discovering that she looks like a haddock.
- Die? I should say not, dear fellow. No Barrymore would allow such a conventional thing to happen to him.

Baudelaire, Charles

- A book is a garden, an orchard, a storehouse, a party, a company by the way, a counselor, a multitude of counselors.
- Any healthy man can go without food for two days - but not without poetry.
- Genius is no more than childhood recaptured at will, childhood equipped now with man's physical means to express itself, and with the analytical mind that enables it to bring order into the sum of experience, involuntarily amassed.

- I consider it useless and tedious to represent what exists, because nothing that exists satisfies me. Nature is ugly, and I prefer the monsters of my fancy to what is positively trivial.
- It is by universal misunderstanding that all agree. For if, by ill luck, people understood each other, they would never agree.
- It is necessary to work, if not from inclination, at least from despair. Everything considered, work is less boring than amusing oneself.
- Poetry and progress are like two ambitious men who hate one another with an instinctive hatred, and when they meet upon the same road, one of them has to give place.
- The world only goes round by misunderstanding.
- We are weighed down, every moment, by the conception and the sensation of Time. And there are but two means of escaping and forgetting this nightmare: pleasure and work. Pleasure consumes us. Work strengthens us. Let us choose.
- There exist only three beings worthy of respect: the priest, the soldier, the poet. To know, to kill, to create.

Beecham, Sir Thomas

- A musicologist is a man who can read music but can't hear it.

- Brass bands are all very well in their place - outdoors and several miles away.

Beecher, Henry Ward

- Books are not made for furniture, but there is nothing else that so beautifully furnishes a house.
- Fear secretes acids; but love and trust are sweet juices.
- It usually takes 100 years to make a law, and then, after it's done its work, it usually takes 100 years to be rid of it.
- Never forget what a man says to you when he is angry.
- Our days are a kaleidoscope. Every instant a change takes place in the contents. New harmonies, new contrasts, new combinations of every sort. Nothing ever happens twice alike. The most familiar people stand each moment in some new relation to each other, to their work, to surrounding objects. The most tranquil house, with the most serene inhabitants, living upon the utmost regularity of system, is yet exemplifying infinite diversities.
- Repentance may begin instantly, but reformation often requires a sphere of years.

- The dog was created especially for children. He is the god of frolic.
- The meanest, most contemptible kind of praise is that which first speaks well of a man, and then qualifies it with a "but".
- We sleep, but the loom of life never stops, and the pattern which was weaving when the sun went down is weaving when it comes up in the morning.
- Where is human nature so weak as in the bookstore?
- You never know till you try to reach them how accessible men are; but you must approach each man by the right door.
- The power of hiding ourselves from one another is mercifully given, for men are wild beasts, and would devour one another but for this protection.
- Every artist dips his brush in his own soul, and paints his own nature into his pictures.

Beerbohm, Max

- No fine work can be done without concentration and self-sacrifice and toil and doubt.
- Nobody ever died of laughter.

- You cannot make a man by standing a sheep on its hind legs. But by standing a flock of sheep in that position you can make a crowd of men.

Benchley, Robert

- A boy can learn a lot from a dog: obedience, loyalty, and the importance of turning around three times before lying down.
- An ardent supporter of the hometown team should go to a game prepared to take offense, no matter what happens.
- Anyone can do any amount of work provided it isn't the work he is supposed to be doing at the moment.
- As for me, except for an occasional heart attack, I feel as young as I ever did.
- Defining and analyzing humor is a pastime of humorless people.
- Drawing on my fine command of the English language, I said nothing.
- Drinking makes such fools of people, and people are such fools to begin with, that it's compounding a felony.
- I can't bring myself to say, 'Well, I guess I'll be

toddling along.' It isn't that I can't toddle. It's just that I can't guess I'll toddle.

- It took me fifteen years to discover that I had no talent for writing, but I couldn't give it up because by that time I was too famous.
- The surest way to make a monkey of a man is to quote him.
- There are two kinds of people in the world, those who believe there are two kinds of people in the world and those who don't.

Bennett, Arnold

- A man of sixty has spent twenty years in bed and over three years in eating.
- Beware of undertaking too much at the start. Be content with quite a little. Allow for accidents. Allow for human nature, especially your own.
- Falsehood often lurks upon the tongue of him, who, by self-praise, seeks to enhance his value in the eyes of others.
- Having once decided to achieve a certain task, achieve it at all costs of tedium and distaste. The gain in self-confidence of having accomplished a tiresome labor is immense.

- The best cure for worry, depression, melancholy, brooding, is to go deliberately forth and try to lift with one's sympathy the gloom of somebody else.

Bevan, Aneurin

- Virtue is its own punishment.
- We know what happens to people who stay in the middle of the road. They get run over.

Bible

Daniel

- Thou art weighed in the balances, and found wanting.

Deuteronomy

- As a man chasteneth his son, so the Lord God chasteneth thee.

Ecclesiastes

- There is no new thing under the sun.

- Whatsoever thy hand findeth to do, do it with thy might.
- The race is not to the swift, nor the battle to the strong.
- For a living dog is better than a dead lion,
- The sleep of a laboring man is sweet.
- Be not righteous overmuch
- It is better to go to the house of mourning than to go to the house of feasting.
- Cast thy bread upon the waters; for thou shalt find it after many days.
- Remember now thy Creator in the days of thy youth.
- Of making many books there is no end; and much study is a weariness of the flesh.
- And the grasshopper shall be a burden.
- Man goeth to his long home.
- Or ever the silver cord be loosed, or the golden bowl be broken, or the pitcher be broken at the fountain, or the wheel broken at the cistern.
- Then shall the dust return to the earth as it was; and the spirit shall return unto God who gave it.
- Vanity of vanities, saith the Preacher; all is vanity.

- He that toucheth pitch shall be defiled therewith.
- He will laugh thee to scorn.
- Be ye angry, and sin not: let not the sun go down upon your wrath.

Hebrews

- For whom the Lord loveth he chasteneth.
- Be not forgetful to entertain strangers, for thereby some have entertained angels unawares.
- For they have sown the wind, and they shall reap the whirlwind.
- And the work of righteousness shall be peace; and the effect of righteousness quietness and assurance for ever.
- Faith is the substance of things hoped for, the evidence of things not seen.

Isaiah

- He is brought as a lamb to the slaughter.
- A little one shall become a thousand, and a small one a strong nation.
- Give unto them beauty for ashes, the oil of joy for mourning.

- We all do fade as a leaf.
- The wolf also shall dwell with the lamb, and the leopard shall lie down with the kid.
- Behold, the nations are as a drop of a bucket, and are counted as the small dust of the balance.
- All flesh is grass.
- A bruised reed shall he not break, and the smoking flax shall he not quench.
- Precept upon precept; line upon line: here a little, and there a little.
- Set thine house in order.
- For if any be a hearer of the word, and not a doer, he is like unto a man beholding his natural face in a glass: for he beholdeth himself, and goeth his way, and straightway forgetteth what manner of man he was.

Jeremiah

- Is there no balm in Gilead? is there no physician there?
- Can the Ethiopian change his skin, or the leopard his spots?
- The Lord gave, and the Lord hath taken away; blessed be the name of the Lord.

Job

- There the wicked cease from troubling, and there the weary be at rest.
- Yet man is born unto trouble, as the sparks fly upward.
- I know that my Redeemer liveth.
- Miserable comforters are ye all.
- I was eyes to the blind, and feet was I to the lame.
- The price of wisdom is above-rubies.
- That mine adversary had written a book.
- Hitherto shalt thou come, but no further; and here shall thy proud waves be stayed.
- Ye shall know the truth, and the truth shall make you free.

John

- Behold the Lamb of God, which taketh away the sin of the world!
- Can there any good thing come out of Nazareth?
- Except a man be born again, he cannot see the kingdom of God.

- The wind bloweth where it listeth.
- He was a burning and a shining light.
- Gather up the fragments that remain, that nothing be lost.
- Judge not according to the appearance.
- Walk while ye have the light, lest darkness come upon you.
- For the poor always ye have with you.
- Let not your heart be troubled.
- In my Father's house are many mansions.
- Greater love hath no man than this, that a man lay down his life for his friends.
- The Philistines be upon thee, Samson.

Judges

- There is death in the pot.

Kings

- A proverb and a by-word among all people,
- A still, small voice.

- How long halt ye between two opinions?
- Behold, there ariseth a little cloud out of the sea, like a man's hand.
- Let not him that girdeth on his harness boast himself as he that putteth it off.
- And now also the ax is laid unto the root of the trees.

Luke

- Physician, heal thyself.
- Go, and do thou likewise.
- But one thing is needful: and Mary hath chosen that good part, which shall not be taken away from her.
- He that is not with me is against me.
- And I will say to my soul, Soul, thou hast much goods laid up for many years; take thine ease, eat, drink, and be merry.
- Let your loins be girded about, and your lights burning.
- Out of thine own mouth will I judge thee.
- For the children of this world are in their generation wiser than the children of light.

- It were better for him that a millstone were hanged about his neck, and he cast into the sea.
- Remember Lot's wife.
- But unto you that fear my name shall the Sun of righteousness arise with healing in his wings.

Malachi

- He that hath ears to hear, let him hear.

Mark

- Where their worm dieth not, and the fire is not quenched.
- My name is Legion.
- Rachel weeping for her children, and would not be comforted, because they are not.

Matthew

- Man shall not live by bread alone.
- The harvest truly is plenteous, but the laborers are few.
- Ye are the salt of the earth: but if the salt have lost his savor, wherewith shall it be salted?

- Ye are the light of the world. A city set upon a hill cannot be hid.
- Where your treasure is, there will your heart be also.
- Ye cannot serve God and Mammon.
- Consider the lilies of the field, how they grow; they toil not, neither do they spin.
- But when thou doest alms, let not thy left hand know what thy right hand doeth.
- Take therefore no thought for the morrow; for the morrow shall take thought for the things of itself. Sufficient unto the day is the evil thereof.
- Neither cast ye your pearls before swine.
- The foxes have holes, and the birds of the air have nests; but the Son of Man hath not where to lay his head.
- Be ye therefore wise as serpents, and harmless as doves.
- But the very hairs of your head are all numbered.
- The tree is known by his fruit.
- Out of the abundance of the heart the mouth speaketh.
- A prophet is not without honor, save in his own country, and in his own house.

- Be of good cheer: it is I; be not afraid.
- It is easier for a camel to go through the eye of a needle than for a rich man to enter into the kingdom of God.
- What therefore God hath joined together let not man put asunder.
- A soft answer turneth away wrath.

Proverbs

- Better is a dinner of herbs where love is, than a stalled ox and hatredtherewith.
- Pride goeth before destruction, and a haughty spirit before a fall.
- The hoary head is a crown of glory.
- A wounded spirit who can bear?
- Train up a child in the way he should go; and when he is old he will not depart from it.
- For riches certainly make themselves wings.
- Yet a little sleep, a little slumber, a little folding of the hands to sleep.
- For thou shalt heap coals of fire upon his head.
- There is a lion in the way; a lion is in the streets.

- Boast not thyself of to-morrow; for thou knowest not what a day may bring forth.
- The wicked flee when no man pursueth.
- They reel to and fro, and stagger like a drunken man, and are at their wit's end.

Psalm

- He giveth his beloved sleep.
- Behold, how good and how pleasant it is for brethren to dwell together in unity!
- For I am fearfully and wonderfully made.
- We hanged our harps on the willows.
- If I forget thee, O Jerusalem, let my right hand forget her cunning.
- Oh, that I had wings like a dove!
- His enemies shall lick the dust.
- Mercy and truth are met together: righteousness and peace have kissed each other.
- We spend our years as a tale that is told.
- My tongue is the pen of a ready writer.
- The lines are fallen unto me in pleasant places.

- Yea, he did fly upon the wings of the wind.
- He maketh me to lie down in green pastures he leadeth me beside the still waters.
- Thy rod and thy staff they comfort me.
- While I was musing the fire burned.
- I have been young, and now am old; yet have I not seen the righteous forsaken, nor his seed begging bread.
- Spreading himself like a green bay tree.
- Be thou faithful unto death.

Revelation

- He shall rule them with a rod of iron.
- I am Alpha and Omega, the beginning and the end, the first and the last.
- For there is no respect of persons with God.

Romans

- For the wages of sin is death.
- And we know that all things work together for good to them that love God.

- Be not wise in your own conceits.
- Therefore if thine enemy hunger, feed him; if he thirst, give him drink: for in so doing thou shalt heap coals of fire on his head.
- Be not overcome of evil, but overcome evil with good.
- The powers that be are ordained of God,
- Love is the fulfilling of the law.
- Render therefore to all their dues.
- Let every man be fully persuaded in his own mind.
- For whither thou goest, I will go; and where thou lodgest, I will lodge: thy people shall be my people, and thy God my God.

Ruth

- Tell it not in Gath; publish it not in the streets of Ashkelon

Samuel

- Saul and Jonathan were lovely and pleasant in their lives, and in their death they were not divided.
- How are the mighty fallen in the midst of the battle!

- Very pleasant hast thou been unto me: thy love to me was wonderful, passing the love of women.
- And Nathan said to David, Thou art the man.
- A man after his own heart.
- Unto the pure all things are pure.

Bierce, Ambrose

- Brain: an apparatus with which we think we think.
- Cabbage: A familiar kitchen-garden vegetable about as large and wise as a man's head.
- Calamities are of two kinds: misfortunes to ourselves, and good fortune to others.
- (I think that I think, therefore I think that I am.)
- In our civilization, and under our republican form of government, intelligence is so highly honored that it is rewarded by exemption from the cares of office.
- Painting: The art of protecting flat surfaces from the weather and exposing them to the critic.
- The covers of this book are too far apart.
- The gambling known as business looks with austere disfavor upon the business known as gambling.

- There is nothing new under the sun but there are lots of old things we don't know.
- To be positive: To be mistaken at the top of one's voice.

Billings, Josh

- A dog is the only thing on earth that loves you more than he loves himself.
- About the most originality that any writer can hope to achieve honestly is to steal with good judgment.
- As scarce as truth is, the supply has always been in excess of the demand.
- Don't take the bull by the horns, take him by the tail; then you can let go when you want to.
- Flattery is like cologne water, to be smelt of, not swallowed.
- It is much easier to repent of sins that we have committed than to repent of those we intend to commit.
- Laughing is the sensation of feeling good all over and showing it principally in one spot.
- One of the greatest victories you can gain over someone is to beat him at politeness.

- Silence is one of the hardest arguments to refute.
- The best way to convince a fool that he is wrong is to let him have his own way.
- The time to pray is not when we are in a tight spot but just as soon as we get out of it.
- There is no revenge so complete as forgiveness.
- As scarce as truth is, the supply has always been in excess of the demand.

Bismarck, Ottovon

- A really great man is known by three signs... generosity in the design, humanity in the execution, moderation in success.
- Laws are like sausages. It's better not to see them being made.
- When a man says he approves of something in principle, it means he hasn't the slightest intention of putting it into practice.
- Beware of sentimental alliances where the consciousness of good deeds is the only compensation for noble sacrifices.
- Politics is the art of the possible.

Brecht, Bertolt

- Because things are the way they are, things will not stay the way they are.
- Why be a man when you can be a success?
- Do not fear death so much, but rather the inadequate life.
- For the villainy of the world is great, and a man has to run his legs off to keep them from being stolen out fom underneath him.

Browne, Sir Thomas

- Be charitable before wealth makes thee covetous.
- Be substantially great in thyself, and more than thou appearest unto others.
- There is surely a piece of divinity in us, something that was before the elements, and owes no homage unto the sun.

Browning , Elizabeth Barrett

- Measure not the work until the day's out and the labor done.
- Since when was genius found respectable?

Browning, Robert

- A minute's success pays the failure of years.
- Ah, but a man's reach should exceed his grasp - or what's a heaven for?
- Grow old along with me the best is yet to be.
- I show you doubt, to prove that faith exists.
- Ignorance is not innocence but sin.
- What's the earth With all its art, verse, music, worth - Compared with love, found, gained, and kept?
- Why comes temptation, but for man to meet and master and crouch beneath his foot, and so be pedestaled in triumph?

Buddha, Gautama

- If you knew what I know about the power of giving, you would not let a single meal pass without sharing it in some way.
- Hatred does not cease in this world by hating, but by not hating; this is an eternal truth.

Burke, Edmund

- All that is necessary for the triumph of evil is that good men do nothing.
- Better be despised for too anxious apprehensions, than ruined by too confident security.
- He who wrestles with us strengthens our nerves and sharpens our skill. Our antagonist is our helper.
- Hypocrisy can afford to be magnificent in its promises; for never intending to go beyond promises; it costs nothing.
- I thought ten thousand swords must have leaped from their scabbards to avenge even a look that threatened her with insult. But the age of chivalry is gone.
- It is the nature of all greatness not to be exact.
- Never despair; but if you do, work on in despair.
- No one could make a greater mistake than he who did nothing because he could do only a little.
- Our patience will achieve more than our force.
- The wise determine from the gravity of the case; the irritable, from sensibility to oppression; the high minded, from disdain and indignation at abusive power in unworthy hands.

- No passion so effectually robs the mind of all its powers of acting and reasoning as fear.
- Good order is the foundation of all things.

Burton, Robert

- Hence it is clear how much more cruel the pen is than the sword.
- Almost in every kingdom the most ancient families have been at first princes' bastards.

Byron, Lord

- A pretty woman is a welcome guest.
- Always laugh when you can. It is cheap medicine.
- For the sword outwears its sheath, And the soul wears out the breast, And the heart must pause for breath, And love itself have rest.
- How sweet and soothing is this hour of calm! I thank thee, night! for thou has chased away these horrid bodements which, amidst the throng, I could not dissipate; and with the blessing of thy benign and quiet influence now will I to my couch, although to rest is almost wronging such a night as this.

- Is the lava of the imagination whose eruption prevents an earthquake.
- Oh! too convincing - dangerously dear - In woman's eye the unanswerable tear!

C

Camus, Albert

- Autumn is a second spring when every leaf is a flower.
- Charm is a way of getting the answer yes without asking a clear question.
- Do not wait for the last judgment. It takes place every day.
- Don't walk in front of me, I may not follow. Don't walk behind me, I may not lead. Walk beside me and be my friend.
- I shall tell you a great secret, my friend. Do not wait for the last judgment, it takes place every day.
- If there is a sin against life, it consists perhaps not so much in despairing of life as in hoping for another life and in eluding the implacable grandeur of this life.
- In the depth of winter, I finally learned that within me there lay an invincible summer.
- Nobody realizes that some people expend tremendous energy merely to be normal.

- There is no fate that cannot be surmounted by scorn.
- Too many have dispensed with generosity in order to practice charity.
- We only know of one duty, and that is to love.
- We rarely confide in those who are better than we are.
- You cannot acquire experience by making experiments. You cannot create experience. You must undergo it.
- Love is the kind of illness that does not spare the inteligent or the dull.
- But in the end one needs more courage to live than to kill himself.
- What is a rebel? A man who says no.
- You know what charm is: a way of getting the answer yes without having asked any clear question.
- All great deeds and all great thoughts have a ridiculous beginning.
- I see many people die because they judge that life is not worth living. I see others paradoxically gettin killed for the ideas or illusions that give them a reason for living (what is called a reason for living is also an excellent reason for dying). I therefore conclude that the meaning of life is the most urgent of questions.

- It is natural to give a clear view of the world after accepting the idea that it must be clear.
- There is but one truly philosophical problem, and that is suicide.
- He who despairs over an event is a coward, but he who holds hope for the human condition is a fool.

Carlyle, Thomas

- A well-written life is almost as rare as a well-spent one.
- All men, if they work not as in the great taskmaster's eye, will work wrong, and work unhappily for themselves and for you.
- Enjoy things which are pleasant; that is not the evil: it is the reducing of our moral self to slavery by them that is.
- Our main business is not to see what lies dimly at a distance but to do what lies clearly at hand.
- Popular opinion is the greatest lie in the world.
- Speech is human, silence is divine, yet also brutish and dead: therefore we must learn both arts.
- That there should one Man die ignorant who had capacity for Knowledge, this I call a tragedy.

- The best effect of any book is that it excites the reader to self-activity.
- The greatest of faults, I should say, is to be conscious of none.
- Under all speech that is good for anything there lies a silence that is better. Silence is deep as Eternity; speech is shallow as Time.
- What we become depends on what we read after all of the professors have finished with us. The greatest university of all is a collection of books.
- Blessed is he who has found his work; let him ask no other blessedness.

Carroll, Lewis

- Everything has got a moral if you can only find it.
- If you don't know where you are going, any road will take you there.
- It's a poor sort of memory that only works backward.
- Sometimes I've believed as many as six impossible things before breakfast.
- Begin at the beginning and go on till you come to the end: then stop.

Cervantes, Miguel De

- A proverb is a short sentence based on long experience.
- Among the attributes of God, although they are all equal, mercy shines with even more brilliancy than justice.
- Be brief, for no discourse can please when too long.
- Delay always breeds danger; and to protract a great design is often to ruin it.
- Everyone is as God has made him, and oftentimes a great deal worse.
- Never stand begging for that which you have the power to earn.
- Short sentences drawn from long experiences.
- The bow cannot always stand bent, nor can human frailty subsist without some lawful recreation.
- Truth indeed rather alleviates than hurts, and will always bear up against falsehood, as oil does above water.
- The most difficult character in comedy is that of a fool, and he must be no simpleton who plays the part.

- I say that good painters imitated nature; but that bad ones vomited it.
- Facts are the enemy of truth.

Chamfort, Nicholas

- An economist is a surgeon with an excellent scalpel and a rough-edged lancet, who operates beautifully on the dead and tortures the living.
- In great affairs men show themselves as they wish to be seen; in small things they show themselves as they are.

Chekhov, Anton

- Man is what he believes.
- Perhaps the feelings that we experience when we are in love represent a normal state. Being in love shows a person who he should be.
- Try to reason about love, and you will lose your reason.
- We shall find peace. We shall hear the angels, we shall see the sky sparkling with diamonds.

Chesterfield, Lord

- Be wiser than other people, if you can, but do not tell them so.
- Choose your pleasures for yourself, and do not let them be imposed upon you.
- He makes people pleased with him by making them first pleased with themselves.
- Know the true value of time; snatch, seize, and enjoy every moment of it. No idleness; no laziness; no procrastination; never put off till tomorrow what you can do today.
- Never seem more learned than the people you are with. Wear your learning like a pocket watch and keep it hidden. Do not pull it out to count the hours, but give the time when you are asked.
- Whatever you do, do it to the purpose; do it thoroughly, not superficially. Go to the bottom of things. Any thing half done, or half known, is in my mind, neither done nor known at all. Nay, worse, for it often misleads.
- Common sense is the best sense I know of.
- Wit is so shining a quality that everybody admires it; most people aim at it, all people fear it, and few love it unless in themselves.

- The knowledge of the world is only to be acquired in the world, and not in a closet.

Chesterton, G. K.

- "My country, right or wrong," is a thing that no patriot would think of saying except in a desperate case. It is like saying, "My mother, drunk or sober."
- A good novel tells us the truth about its hero; but a bad novel tells us the truth about its author.
- An adventure is only an inconvenience rightly considered. An inconvenience is an adventure wrongly considered.
- Art, like morality, consists of drawing the line somewhere.
- By a curious confusion, many modern critics have passed from the proposition that a masterpiece may be unpopular to the other proposition that unless it is unpopular it cannot be a masterpiece.
- Don't ever take a fence down until you know the reason it was put up.
- Fallacies do not cease to be fallacies because they become fashions.
- I believe in getting into hot water; it keeps you clean.

- I owe my success to having listened respectfully to the very best advice, and then going away and doing the exact opposite.
- I say that a man must be certain of his morality for the simple reason that he has to suffer for it.
- If there were no God, there would be no Atheists.
- It is not bigotry to be certain we are right; but it is bigotry to be unable to imagine how we might possibly have gone wrong.
- Journalism largely consists of saying 'Lord Jones is Dead' to people who never knew that Lord Jones was alive.
- Man seems to be capable of great virtues but not of small virtues; capable of defying his torturer but not of keeping his temper.
- Music with dinner is an insult both to the cook and the violinist.
- Poets have been mysteriously silent on the subject of cheese.
- The Bible tells us to love our neighbors, and also to love our enemies; probably because they are generally the same people.
- The most astonishing thing about miracles is that they happen.
- The people who are the most bigoted are the people who have no convictions at all.

- The thing I hate about an argument is that it always interrupts a discussion.
- There is a great deal of difference between an eager man who wants to read a book and the tired man who wants a book to read.
- To have a right to do a thing is not at all the same as to be right in doing it.
- You can only find truth with logic if you have already found truth without it.
- There are no wise few. Every aristocracy that has ever existed has behaved, in all essential points, exactly like a small mob.
- All slang is a metaphor, and all metaphor is poetry.
- Literature is a luxury; fiction is a necessity.
- The rich are the scum of the earth in every country.
- There is no such thing on earth as an uninteresting subject; the only thing that can exist is an uninterested person.
- The poet only asks to get his head into the heavens. It is the logician who seeks to get the heavens into his head. And it is his head that splits.
- Tradition means giving votes to the most obscure of all classes, our ancestors. It is the democracy of the dead. Tradition refuses to submit to the small and arrogant oligarchy of those who merely happen to be walking about.

- The men who really believe in themselves are all in lunatic asylums.
- It isn't that they can't see the solution. It is that they can't see the problem.
- He may be mad, but there's method in his madness. There nearly always is method in madness. It's what drives men mad, being methodical.
- But a somewhat more liberal and sympathetic examination of mankind will convince us that the cross is even older than the gibbet, that voluntary suffering was before and independent of compulsory; and in short that in most important matters a man has always been free to ruin himself if he chose.

Churchill, Sir Winston

- A fanatic is one who can't change his mind and won't change the subject.
- A love for tradition has never weakened a nation, indeed it has strengthened nations in their hour of peril.
- All great things are simple, and many can be expressed in single words: freedom, justice, honor, duty, mercy, hope.

- Although prepared for martyrdom, I preferred that it be postponed.
- An appeaser is one who feeds a crocodile, hoping it will eat him last.
- Broadly speaking, the short words are the best, and the old words best of all.
- Every day you may make progress. Every step may be fruitful. Yet there will stretch out before you an ever-lengthening, ever-ascending, ever-improving path. You know you will never get to the end of the journey. But this, so far from discouraging, only adds to the joy and glory of the climb.
- From now on, ending a sentence with a preposition is something up with which I will not put.
- He has all the virtues I dislike and none of the vices I admire.
- History will be kind to me for I intend to write it.
- I cannot pretend to feel impartial about colours. I rejoice with the brilliant ones and am genuinely sorry for the poor browns.
- I have always felt that a politician is to be judged by the animosities he excites among his opponents.
- I like pigs. Dogs look up to us. Cats look down on us. Pigs treat us as equals.

- It has been said that democracy is the worst form of government except all the others that have been tried.
- It is a mistake to try to look too far ahead. The chain of destiny can only be grasped one link at a time.
- It's not enough that we do our best; sometimes we have to do what's required.
- Men occasionally stumble over the truth, but most of them pick themselves up and hurry off as if nothing ever happened.
- Never hold discussions with the monkey when the organ grinder is in the room.
- Personally I'm always ready to learn, although I do not always like being taught.
- Success is the ability to go from one failure to another with no loss of enthusiasm.
- The price of greatness is responsibility.
- The reserve of modern assertions is sometimes pushed to extremes, in which the fear of being contradicted leads the writer to strip himself of almost all sense and meaning.
- There are a terrible lot of lies going around the world, and the worst of it is half of them are true.
- To build may have to be the slow and laborious task of years. To destroy can be the thoughtless act of a single day.

- We make a living by what we get, we make a life by what we give.
- When I am abroad, I always make it a rule never to criticize or attack the government of my own country. I make up for lost time when I come home.
- When the eagles are silent, the parrots begin to jabber.
- Don't talk to me about naval tradition. It's nothing but rum, sodomy and the lash.
- "Courage is what it takes to stand up and speak, Courage is also what it takes to sit down and listen."
- We shall not fail or falter; we shall not weaken or tire...Give us the tools and we will finish the job.
- The British nation is unique in this respect. They are the only people who like to be told how bad things are, who like to be told the worst.
- I would say to the House, as I said to those who have joined this Government: 'I have nothing to offer but blood, toil, tears, and sweat."
- Many forms of Government have been tried, and will be tried in this world of sin and woe. No one pretends that democracy is perfect or all-wise. Indeed, it has been said that democracy is the worst form of government except all those other forms that have been tried from time to time.

- So they [the Government] go on in strange paradox, decided only to be undecided, resolved to be irresolute, adamant for drift, solid for fluidity, all-powerful to be impotent.

- It is a good thing for an uneducated man to read books of quotations.

- I am prepared to meet my Maker. Whether my Maker is prepared for the great ordeal of meeting me is another matter.

- I am reminded of the professor who, in his declining hours, was asked by his devoted pupils for his final counsel. He replied, 'Verify your quotations.'

- I cannot forecast to you the action of Russia. It is a riddle wrapped in a mystery inside an enigma: but perhaps there is a key. That key is Russian national interest.

- Here is the answer which I will give to President Roosevelt... We shall not fail or falter; we shall not weaken or tire. Neither the sudden shock of battle nor the long-drawn trials of vigilance and exertion will wear us down. Give us the tools and we will finish the job.

- It is a good thing for an uneducated man to read books of quotations. Bartlett's Familiar Quotations is an admirable work, and I studied it intently. The quotations when engraved upon the memory give you good thoughts. They also make you anxious to read the authors and look for more.

- One day President Roosevelt told me that he was asking publicly for suggestions about what the war should be called. I said at once 'The Unnecessary War'.
- The empires of the future are the empires of the mind.
- For myself I am an optimist - it does not seem to be much use being anything else.
- From Stettin in the Baltic to Trieste in the Adriatic an iron curtain has descended across the Continent.
- Now this is not the end. It is not even the beginning of the end. But it is, perhaps, the end of the beginning.
- We shall show mercy, but we shall not ask for it.
- A love of tradition has never weakened a nation, indeed it has strengthened nations in their hour of peril; but the new view must come, the world must roll forward.
- Never give in—never, never, never, never, in nothing great or small, large or petty, never give in except to convictions of honour and good sense. Never yield to force; never yield to the apparently overwhelming might of the enemy.

Cocteau, Jean

- Art is science made clear.
- The worst tragedy for a poet is to be admired through being misunderstood.
- We must believe in luck. For how else can we explain the success of those we don't like?
- The instinct of nearly all societies is to lock up anybody who is truly free. First, society begins by trying to beat you up. If this fails, they try to poison you. If this fails too, they finish by loading honors on your head.
- The actual tragedies of life bear no relation to one's preconceived ideas. In the event, one is always bewildered by their simplicity, their grandeur of design, and by that element of the bizzare which seems inherent in them.

Coleridge, Samuel Taylor

- A poet ought not to pick nature's pocket. Let him borrow, and so borrow as to repay by the very act of borrowing. Examine nature accurately, but write from recollection, and trust more to the imagination than the memory.
- Advice is like snow; the softer it falls, the longer it dwells upon, and the deeper it sinks into, the mind.

- I have seen gross intolerance shown in support of tolerance.
- If you would stand well with a great mind, leave him with a favorable impression of yourself; if with a little mind, leave him with a favorable impression of himself.
- Oh sleep! It is a gentle thing, Beloved from pole to pole.
- Only the wise possess ideas; the greater part of mankind are possessed by them.
- There is no such thing as a worthless book though there are some far worse than worthless; no book that is not worth preserving, if its existence may be tolerated; as there may be some men whom it may be proper to hang, but none should be suffered to starve.
- What is an epigram? A dwarfish whole, its body brevity, and wit its soul.
- Works of imagination should be written in very plain language; the more purely imaginative they are the more necessary it is to be plain.

Cromwell, Oliver

- I beseech you, in the bowels of Christ, think it possible you may be mistaken.

- Do not trust to the cheering, for those very persons would shout as much if you and I were going to be hanged.
- I had rather have a plain, russetcoated Captain, that knows what he fights for, and loves what he knows, than that which you call a Gentleman and is nothing else.

D

Da Vinci, Leonardo

- As a well-spent day brings happy sleep, so life well used brings happy death.
- Patience serves as a protection against wrongs as clothes do against cold. For if you put on more clothes as the cold increases, it will have no power to hurt you. So in like manner you must grow in patience when you meet with great wrongs, and they will then be powerless to vex your mind.
- Study without desire spoils the memory, and it retains nothing that it takes in.
- You do ill if you praise, but worse if you censure, what you do not understand.
- Intellectual passion dries out sensuality.
- Iron rusts from disuse; stagnant water loses its purity and in cold weather becomes frozen; even so does inaction sap the vigor of the mind.

Dickens, Charles

- A man who could build a church, as one may say, by squinting at a sheet of paper.

- Accidents will occur in the best regulated families.
- I do not know the American gentleman, god forgive me for putting two such words together.
- Minds, like bodies, will often fall into a pimpled, ill-conditioned state from mere excess of comfort.
- No one is useless in this world who lightens the burdens of another.
- Reflect on your present blessings, of which every man has many; not on your past misfortunes, of which all men have some.
- Subdue your appetites, my dears, and you've conquered human nature.
- Train up a fig tree in the way it should go, and when you are old sit under the shade of it.
- With affection beaming out of one eye, and calculation shining out of the other.
- It is a far, far better thing that I do, than I have ever done; it is a far, far better rest that I go to, than I have ever known.
- It was the best of times, it was the worst of times, it was the age of wisdom, it was the age of foolishness, it was the epoch of belief, it was the epoch of incredulity, it was the season of Light, it was the season of Darkness, it was the spring of hope, it was the winter of despair, we had everything before us, we had nothing before us, we were all going direct to heaven, we were all doing direct the other way - in short, the period was so far like the present period, that some of its noisiest authorities insisted on its being received, for good or for evil, in the superlative degree of comparison only.

- Annual income twenty pounds, annual expenditure nineteen six, result happiness. Annual income twenty pounds, annual expenditure twenty pound ought and six, result misery.
- We need never be ashamed of our tears.

Didion, Joan

- I write entirely to find out what I'm thinking, what I'm looking at, what I see and what it means. What I want and what I fear.
- Character - the willingness to accept responsibility for one's own life - is the source from which self respect springs.
- To have that sense of one's intrinsic worth... is potentially to have everything...

Disraeli, Benjamin

- A precedent embalms a principle.
- As a general rule the most successful man in life is the man who has the best information.
- Bore: one who has the power of speech but not the capacity for conversation.
- Justice is truth in action.

- Cleanliness and order are not matters of instinct; they are matters of education, and like most great things, you must cultivate a taste for them.
- Great services are not canceled by one act or by one single error.
- Grief is the agony of an instant, the indulgence of grief the blunder of a life.
- He was one of those men who think that the world can be saved by writing a pamphlet.
- I repeat...that all power is a trust; that we are accountable for its exercise; that from the people, and for the people all springs, and all must exist.
- Ignorance never settles a question.
- In a progressive country change is constant; ...change... is inevitable.
- Individuals may form communities, but it is institutions alone that can create a nation.
- It is knowledge that influences and equalizes the social condition of man; that gives to all, however different their political position, passions which are in common, and enjoyments which are universal.
- My idea of an agreeable person is a person who agrees with me.
- Never apologize for showing feeling. When you do so, you apologize for truth.

- Next to knowing when to seize an opportunity, the most important thing in life is to know when to forego an advantage.
- No government can be long secure without formidable opposition.
- Nurture your mind with great thoughts; to believe in the heroic makes heroes.
- The best way to become acquainted with a subject is to write a book about it.
- The difference of race is one of the reasons why I fear war may always exist; because race implies difference, difference implies superiority, and superiority leads to predominance.
- The greatest good you can do for another is not just share your riches, but to reveal to him his own.
- The hare-brained chatter of irresponsible frivolity.
- The magic of first love is our ignorance that it can ever end.
- The more extensive a man's knowledge of what has been done, the greater will be his power of knowing what to do.
- The most dangerous strategy is to jump a chasm in two leaps.
- The secret of success is constancy of purpose.

- The wisdom of the wise, and the experience of ages, may be preserved by quotation.
- There are three kinds of lies: lies, damned lies, and statistics.
- What we anticipate seldom occurs; what we least expected generally happens.
- When men are pure, laws are useless; when men are corrupt, laws are broken.
- When we would prepare the mind by a forcible appeal, an opening quotation is a symphony preluding on the chords those tones we are about to harmonize.
- I am a Conservative to preserve all that is good in our constitution, a Radical to remove all that is bad. I seek to preserve property and to respect order, and I equally decry the appeal to the passions of the many or the prejudices of the few.
- A conservative government is an organized hypocrisy.
- Change is inevitable. In a progressive country change is constant.
- How much easier it is to be critical than to be correct.
- To be conscious that you are ignorant is a great step to knowledge.

Donne, John

- Death be not proud, though some have called thee Mighty and dreadfull, for thou art not so, For, those, whom thou thinkst, thou dost overthrow, die not, poor death, nor yet canst thou kill me.
- No man is an Island, intire of itselfe; every man is a peece of the Continent, a part of the maine...
- No man is an Island, entire of itself; every man is a piece of the Continent, a part of the main; if a clod be washed away by the sea, Europe is the less, as well as if a promontory were, as well as if a manor of thy friends or of thine own were; any man's death diminishes me, because I am involved in Mankind; And therefore never send to know for whom the bell tolls; It tolls for thee.

Dylan, Bob

- He not busy being born is busy dying.
- I think of a hero as someone who understands the degree of responsibility that comes with his freedom.
- If the point is sharp, and the arrow is swift, it can pierce through the dust no matter how thick.

- Some people feel the rain. Others just get wet.
- What's money? A man is a success if he gets up in the morning and goes to bed at night and in between does what he wants to do.
- When you feel in your gut what you are and then dynamically pursue it - don't back down and don't give up - then you're going to mystify a lot of folks.
- Everything passes. Everything changes. Just do what you think you should do.
- The picture you have in your mind of what you're about will come true.
- When you ain't got nothin', you got nothin' to lose.
- You don't need a weather man to know which way the wind blows.
- Swallow your pride, you will not die, it's not poison.

E

Einstein , Albert

- Before God we are all equally wise - and equally foolish.
- Do not worry about your difficulties in Mathematics. I can assure you mine are still greater.
- Ethical axioms are found and tested not very differently from the axioms of science. Truth is what stands the test of experience.
- Every day I remind myself that my inner and outer life are based on the labors of other men, living and dead, and that I must exert myself in order to give in the same measure as I have received and am still receiving.
- Few people are capable of expressing with equanimity opinions which differ from the prejudices of their social environment. Most people are even incapable of forming such opinions.
- I never think of the future - it comes soon enough.
- If I had only known, I would have been a locksmith.

- Gravitation cannot be held responsible for people falling in love. How on earth can you explain in terms of chemistry and physics so important a biological phenomenon as first love? Put your hand on a stove for a minute and it seems like an hour. Sit with that special girl for an hour and it seems like a minute. That's relativity.
- I know not with what weapons World War III will be fought, but World War IV will be fought with sticks and stones.
- If you are out to describe the truth, leave elegance to the tailor.
- Imagination is more important than knowledge...
- It is a miracle that curiosity survives formal education.
- Laws alone can not secure freedom of expression; in order that every man present his views without penalty there must be spirit of tolerance in the entire population.
- My religion consists of a humble admiration of the illimitable superior spirit who reveals himself in the slight details we are able to perceive with our frail and feeble mind.
- Nothing will benefit human health and increase the chances for survival of life on Earth as much as the evolution to a vegetarian diet.

- Only two things are infinite, the universe and human stupidity, and I'm not sure about the former.
- Reading, after a certain age, diverts the mind too much from its creative pursuits. Any man who reads too much and uses his own brain too little falls into lazy habits of thinking.
- The ideals which have lighted my way, and time after time have given me new courage to face life cheerfully, have been Kindness, Beauty, and Truth. The trite subjects of human efforts, possessions, outward success, luxury have always seemed to me contemptible.
- The important thing is not to stop questioning.
- The important thing is not to stop questioning. Curiosity has its own reason for existing. One cannot help but be in awe when he contemplates the mysteries of eternity, of life, of the marvelous structure of reality. It is enough if one tries merely to comprehend a little of this mystery every day. Never lose a holy curiosity.
- The most beautiful experience we can have is the mysterious.
- The most beautiful thing we can experience is the mysterious. It is the source of all true art and science.

- The most incomprehensible thing about the world is that it is at all comprehensible.
- The release of atomic energy has not created a new problem. It has merely made more urgent the necessity of solving an existing one.
- The secret to creativity is knowing how to hide your sources.
- To punish me for my contempt for authority, fate made me an authority myself.
- Too many of us look upon Americans as dollar chasers. This is a cruel libel, even if it is reiterated thoughtlessly by the Americans themselves.
- Truth is what stands the test of experience.
- Try not to become a man of success but rather to become a man of value.
- We should take care not to make the intellect our god; it has, of course, powerful muscles, but no personality.
- Yes, we have to divide up our time like that, between our politics and our equations. But to me our equations are far more important, for politics are only a matter of present concern. A mathematical equation stands forever.
- As far as the laws of mathematics refer to reality, they are not certain; and as far as they are certain, they do not refer to reality.

- Science without religion is lame, religion without science is blind.
- Everything that is really great and inspiring is created by the individual who can labor in freedom.
- It is the duty of every citizen according to his best capacities to give validity to his convictions in political affairs.
- Common sense is the collection of prejudices acquired by age eighteen.
- Everything should be made as simple as possible, but not one bit simpler.
- If the facts don't fit the theory, change the facts.
- Insanity: doing the same thing over and over again and expecting different results.
- Not everything that can be counted counts, and not everything that counts can be counted.
- Reality is merely an illusion, albeit a very persistent one.
- The hardest thing in the world to understand is the income tax.
- The significant problems we have cannot be solved at the same level of thinking with which we created them.

- Whoever undertakes to set himself up as a judge of Truth and Knowledge is shipwrecked by the laughter of the Gods.
- You cannot simultaneously prevent and prepare for war.
- At any rate, I am convinced that He [God] does not play dice.
- If A is success in life, then A equals x plus y plus z. Work is x; y is play; and z is keeping your mouth shut.
- Great spirits have always encountered opposition from mediocre minds. The mediocre mind is incapable of understanding the man who refuses to bow blindly to conventional prejudices and chooses instead to express his opinions courageously and honestly.
- The unleashed power of the atom has changed everything save our modes of thinking and we thus drift toward unparalleled catastrophe.
- When you look at yourself from a universal standpoint, something inside always reminds or informs you that there are bigger and better things to worry about.
- You see, wire telegraph is a kind of a very, very long cat. You pull his tail in New York and his head is meowing in Los Angeles. Do you understand this? And radio operates exactly the same way: you send signals here, they receive them there. The only difference is that there is no cat.

Eisenhower, Dwight D.

- A sense of humor is part of the art of leadership, of getting along with people, of getting things done.
- An intellectual is a man who takes more words than necessary to tell more than he knows.
- Before all else, we seek, upon our common labor as a nation, the blessings of Almighty God.
- Don't join the book burners. Don't think you're going to conceal faults by concealing evidence that they ever existed. Don't be afraid to go in your library and read every book...
- I can think of nothing more boring for the American people than to have to sit in their living rooms for a whole half hour looking at my face on their television screens.
- I like to believe that people in the long run are going to do more to promote peace than our governments. Indeed, I think that people want peace so much that one of these days governments had better get out of the way and let them have it.
- I would rather try to persuade a man to go along, because once I have persuaded him he will stick. If I scare him, he will stay just as long as he is scared, and then he is gone.

- In preparing for battle I have always found that plans are useless, but planning is indispensable.
- May we, in our dealings with all the peoples of the earth, ever speak the truth and serve justice.
- There is nothing wrong with America that the faith, love of freedom, intelligence and energy of her citizens cannot cure.
- Things are more like they are now than they ever were before.
- Though force can protect in emergency, only justice, fairness, consideration and co-operation can finally lead men to the dawn of eternal peace.
- When you appeal to force, there's one thing you must never do - lose.
- When you are in any contest you should work as if there were - to the very last minute - a chance to lose it.
- Every gun that is made, every warship launched, every rocket fired signifies, in the final sense, a theft from those who hunger and are not fed, those who are cold and not clothed. This world in arms is not spending money alone. It is spending the sweat of its laborers, the genius of its scientists, the hopes of its children. This is not a way of life at all in any true sense. Under the cloud of threatening war, it is humanity hanging from a cross of iron.

- A people that values its privileges above its principles soon loses both.
- Farming looks mighty easy when your plow is a pencil, and you're a thousand miles from the corn field.
- Don't think you are going to conceal thoughts by concealing evidence that they ever existed.
- What counts is not necessarily the size of the dog in the fight - it's the size of the fight in the dog.
- We succeed only as we identify in life, or in war, or in anything else, a single overriding objective, and make all other considerations bend to that one objective.

Eliot, George

- Be courteous, be obliging, but don't give yourself over to be melted down for the benefit of the tallow trade.
- Blessed is the influence of one true, loving human soul on another.
- Blessed is the man who, having nothing to say, abstains from giving wordy evidence of the fact.
- One must be poor to know the luxury of giving.
- It's never too late to be who you might have been.

- I think I should have no other mortal wants, if I could always have plenty of music. It seems to infuse strength into my limbs and ideas into my brain. Life seems to go on without effort, when I am filled with music.
- I'm proof against that word failure. I've seen behind it. The only failure a man ought to fear is failure of cleaving to the purpose he sees to be best.
- Ignorance gives one a large range of probabilities.
- The golden moments in the stream of life rush past us and we see nothing but sand; the angels come to visit us, and we only know them when they are gone.
- The important work of moving the world forward does not wait to be done by perfect men.
- The reward of one duty is the power to fulfill another.
- The strongest principle of growth lies in human choice.
- There's folks 'ud stand on their heads and then say the fault was i' their boots.
- We are all apt to believe what the world believes about us.
- What greater thing is there for two human souls than to feel that they are joined... to strengthen each other... to be one with each other in silent unspeakable memories.

- Miss Brooke had that kind of beauty which seems to be thrown into relief by poor dress.
- Animals are such agreeable friends - they ask no questions, they pass no criticisms.
- The scornful nostril and the high head gather not the odors that lie on the track of truth.
- Some people did what their neighbors did so that if any lunatics were at large, one might know and avoid them.
- What we call our despair is often only the painful eagerness of unfed hope.
- Our deeds are like children that are born to us; they live and act apart from our own will. Nay, children may be strangled, but deeds never: they have an indestructible life both in and out of our consciousness.
- Every man who is not a monster, mathematician or a mad philosopher, is the slave of some woman or other.
- Nothing is so good as it seems beforehand.
- There is no feeling, except the extremes of fear and grief, that does not find relief in music.

Eliot , T. S.

- Humankind cannot stand very much reality.

- Humor is also a way of saying something serious.
- I take as metaphysical poetry that in which what is ordinarily apprehensible only by thought is brought within the grasp of feeling, or that in which what is ordinarily only felt is transformed into thought without ceasing to be feeling.
- Some editors are failed writers, but so are most writers.
- Success is relative. It is what we can make of the mess we have made of things.
- The last temptation is the greatest treason: to do the right deed for the wrong reason.
- Whatever you think, be sure it is what you think; whatever you want, be sure that is what you want; whatever you feel, be sure that is what you feel.
- Poetry is not a turning loose of emotion, but an escape from emotion; it is not the expression of personality, but an escape from personality. But, of course, only those who have personality and emotions know what it means to want to escape from these things.
- We shall not cease from exploration. And the end of all our exploring will be to arrive where we started and know the place for the first time.
- Between the desire And the spasm Between the potency And the existence Between the essence And the descent Falls the Shadow

- Between the idea And the reality Between the motion And the act Falls the Shadow
- This is the way the world ends This is the way the world ends This is the way the world ends Not with a bang but a whimper.

Ellis, Havelock

- It is only the great men who are truly obscene. If they had not dared to be obscene, they could never have dared to be great.
- The place where optimism most flourishes is the lunatic asylum.
- Thinking in its lower grades, is comparable to paper money, and in its higher forms it is a kind of poetry.
- What we call 'Progress' is the exchange of one nuisance for another nuisance.
- The sun, the moon and the stars would have disappeared long ago, had they happened to be within reach of predatory human hands.
- The absence of flaw in beauty is itself a flaw.
- The more rapidly a civilization progresses, the sooner it dies for another to rise in its place.

Emerson, Ralph Waldo

- A friend is one before whom I may think aloud.
- A hero is no braver than an ordinary man, but he is braver five minutes longer.
- A man of genius is privileged only as far as he is genius. His dullness is as insupportable as any other dullness.
- All I have seen teaches me to trust the Creator for all I have not seen.
- All our progress is an unfolding, like a vegetable bud. You have first an instinct, then an opinion, then a knowledge as the plant has root, bud, and fruit. Trust the instinct to the end, though you can render no reason.
- As we grow old…the beauty steals inward.
- Be not the slave of your own past. Plunge into the sublime seas, dive deep and swim far, so you shall com back with self-respect, with new power, with an advanced experience that shall explain and overlook the old.
- Beware when the great God lets loose a thinker on this planet.
- Character is higher than intellect… A great soul will be strong to live, as well as to think.

- Children are all foreigners.
- Colleges hate geniuses, just as convents hate saints.
- Conversation is an art in which a man has all mankind for his competitors, for it is that which all are practising every day while they live.
- Democracy becomes a government of bullies tempered by editors.
- Do not go where the path may lead, go instead where there is no path and leave a trail.
- Don't be too timid and squeamish about your actions. All life is an experiment. The more experiments you make the better.
- Don't waste yourself in rejection, nor bark against the bad, but chant the beauty of the good.
- Every great and commanding moment in the annals of the world is the triumph of some enthusiasm.
- Every hero becomes a bore at last.
- Every sweet has its sour; every evil its good.
- Finish each day and be done with it. You have done what you could.
- Give all to love; obey thy heart.
- God enters by a private door into every individual.

- He has not learned the lesson of life who does not every day surmount a fear.
- I awoke this morning with devout thanksgiving for my friends, the old and the new.
- I hate quotations. Tell me what you know.
- I pack my trunk, embrace my friends, embark on the sea, and at last wake up in Naples, and there beside me is the Stern Fact, the Sad Self, unrelenting, identical, that I fled from.
- If I have lost confidence in myself, I have the universe against me.
- Insist on yourself; never imitate... Every great man is unique.
- Let not a man guard his dignity, but let his dignity guard him.
- Live in the sunshine, swim the sea, drink the wild air...
- Make the most of yourself, for that is all there is of you.
- Make yourself necessary to somebody. Do not make life hard to any.
- Money, which represents the prose of life, and which is hardly spoken of in parlors without an apology, is, in its effects and laws, as beautiful as roses.

- Nature magically suits a man to his fortunes, by making them the fruit of his character.
- No great man ever complains of want of opportunity.
- None of us will ever accomplish anything excellent or commanding except when he listens to this whisper which is heard by him alone.
- Nothing can bring you peace but yourself.
- Nothing great was ever achieved without enthusiasm.
- Nothing is at last sacred but the integrity of your own mind.
- Our chief want in life is somebody who shall make us do what we can.
- Our knowledge is the amassed thought and experience of innumerable minds.
- People seem not to see that their opinion of the world is also a confession of their character.
- Shallow men believe in luck. Strong men believe in cause and effect.
- That which we persist in doing becomes easier, not that the task itself has become easier, but that our ability to perform it has improved.
- The adventitious beauty of poetry may be felt in the greater delight with a verse given in a happy quotation than in the poem.

- The ancestor of every action is a thought.
- The end of the human race will be that it will eventually die of civilization.
- The essence of all jokes, of all comedy, seems to be an honest or well intended halfness; a non performance of that which is pretended to be performed, at the same time that one is giving loud pledges of performance. The balking of the intellect, is comedy and it announces itself in the pleasant spasms we call laughter.
- The key to every man is his thought. Sturdy and defying though he look, he has a helm which he obeys, which is the idea after which all his facts are classified. He can only be reformed by showing him a new idea which commands his own.
- The life of man is the true romance, which when it is valiantly conduced, will yield the imagination a higher joy than any fiction.
- The louder he talked of his honor, the faster we counted our spoons.
- The measure of a master is his success in bringing all men around to his opinion twenty years later.
- The only gift is a portion of thyself.
- The only way to have a friend is to be one.
- The ornament of a house is the friends who frequent it.

- The peril of every fine faculty is the delight of playing with it for pride. Talent is commonly developed at the expense of character, and the greater it grows, the more is the mischief. Talent is mistaken for genius, a dogma or system for truth, ambition for greatest, ingenuity for poetry, sensuality for art.
- The world belongs to the energetic.
- There are many things of which a wise man might wish to be ignorant.
- There is no den in the wide world to hide a rogue. Commit a crime and the earth is made of glass. Commit a crime, and it seems as if a coat of snow fell on the ground, such as reveals in the woods the track of every partridge, and fox, and squirrel.
- This time, like all times, is a very good one, if we but know what to do with it.
- Those who cannot tell what they desire or expect, still sigh and struggle with indefinite thoughts and vast wishes.
- Tis the good reader that makes the good book.
- Trust your instinct to the end, though you can render no reason.
- Truth is beautiful, without doubt; but so are lies.
- We all boil at different degrees.

- We do what we must, and call it by the best names.
- What you do speaks so loud that I cannot hear what you say.
- When you strike at a king, you must kill him.
- Whoever is open, loyal, true; of humane and affable demeanour; honourable himself, and in his judgement of others; faithful to his word as to law, and faithful alike to God and man....such a man is a true gentleman.
- Whoso would be a man must be a nonconformist.
- Work and acquire, and thou hast chained the wheel of Chance.
- Hitch your wagon to a star.
- In every work of genius we recognize our own rejected thoughts; they come back to us with a certain alienated majesty.
- Speak what you think today in hard words and tomorrow speak what tomorrow thinks in hard words again, though it contradict every thing you said today.
- Nothing astonishes men so much as common sense and plain dealing.
- Sometimes a scream is better than a thesis.
- To be great is to be misunderstood.

- Finish each day and be done with it. You have done what you could. Some blunders and absurdities no doubt crept in; forget them as soon as you can. Tomorrow is a new day; begin it well and serenely and with too high a spirit to be encumbered with your old nonsense.
- What lies behind us and what lies before us are tiny matters compared to what lies within us.
- He who is in love is wise and is becoming wiser, sees newly every time he looks at the object beloved, drawing from it with his eyes and his mind those virtues which it possesses.
- Trust men and they will be true to you; treat them greatly, and they will show themselves great.
- Immortality. I notice that as soon as writers broach this question they begin to quote. I hate quotation. Tell me what you know.
- When a whole nation is roaring Patriotism at the top of its voice, I am fain to explore the cleanness of its hands and purity of its heart.
- The best effect of fine persons is felt after we have left their presence.
- Next to the originator of a good sentence is the first quoter of it.
- Every artist was first an amateur.
- In the highest civilization, the book is still the highest delight. He who has once known its satisfactions is provided with a resource against calamity.

F

Fielding, Henry

- A newspaper consists of just the same number of words, whether there be any news in it or not.
- A truly elegant taste is generally accompanied with excellency of heart.
- Adversity is the trial of principle. Without it a man hardly knows whether he is honest or not.
- He that can heroically endure adversity will bear prosperity with equal greatness of the soul; for the mind that cannot be dejected by the former is not likely to be transported without the latter.
- Make money your god and it will plague you like the devil.
- Now, in reality, the world have paid too great a compliment to critics, and have imagined them to be men of much greater profundity than they really are.

Fitzgerald, F. Scott

- At 18 our convictions are hills from which we look; At 45 they are caves in which we hide.
- In a real dark night of the soul it is always three o'clock in the morning, day after day.
- The test of a first-rate intelligence is the ability to hold two opposed ideas in the mind at the same time, and still retain the ability to function.
- Sometimes it is harder to deprive oneself of a pain than of a pleasure.

Fleming, Ian

- I shall not waste my days in trying to prolong them.
- A horse is dangerous at both ends and uncomfortable in the middle.

Ford, Henry

- An idealist is a person who helps other people to be prosperous.
- History is more or less bunk.

- I am looking for a lot of men who have an infinite capacity to not know what can't be done.
- Nothing is particularly hard if you divide it into small jobs.
- People can have the Model T in any colour—so long as it's black.
- There is one rule for the industrialist and that is: Make the best quality of goods possible at the lowest cost possible, paying the highest wages possible.
- You can't build a reputation on what you are going to do.
- If you think you can do a thing or think you can't do a thing, you're right.
- History is more or less bunk. It's tradition. We don't want tradition. We want to live in the present and the only history that is worth a tinker's damn is the history we made today.

Franklin, Benjamin

- A countryman between two lawyers is like a fish between two cats.
- A good conscience is a continual Christmas.
- A slip of the foot you may soon recover, but a slip of the tongue you may never get over.

- All human situations have their inconveniences. We feel those of the present but neither see nor feel those of the future; and hence we often make troublesome changes without amendment, and frequently for the worse.
- All would live long, but none would be old.
- An investment in knowledge always pays the best interest.
- Anger is never without Reason, but seldom with a good One.
- At 20 years of age the will reigns, at 30 the wit, at 40 the judgment.
- Be civil to all; sociable to many; familiar with few; friend to one; enemy to none.
- Be slow in choosing a friend, slower in changing.
- Beware of the young doctor and the old barber.
- Do not anticipate trouble, or worry about what may never happen. Keep in the sunlight.
- Drive thy business or it will drive thee.
- Early to bed and early to rise makes a man healthy, wealthy, and wise.
- Educate your children to self-control, to the habit of holding passion and prejudice and evil tendencies subject to an upright and reasoning will, and you have done much to abolish misery from their future and crimes from society.

- Employ thy time well, if thou meanest to get leisure.
- Energy and persistence conquer all things.
- Genius without education is like silver in the mine.
- Glass, china and reputation are easily cracked, and never well mended.
- God heals, and the doctor takes the fees.
- Having been poor is no shame, but being ashamed of it, is.
- He is ill clothed that is bare of virtue.
- He that blows the coals in quarrels that he has nothing to do with, has no right to complain if the sparks fly in his face.
- He that can have patience can have what he will.
- He that falls in love with himself will have no rivals.
- He that is good for making excuses is seldom good for anything else.
- He that is of the opinion money will do everything may well be suspected of doing everything for money.
- He that lives upon hope will die fasting.
- He that would live in peace and at ease, must not speak all he knows nor judge all he sees.

- Hide not your talents, they for use were made. What's a sun-dial in the shade?
- How many observe Christ's birthday! How few, his precepts! O! 'tis easier to keep Holidays than Commandments.
- I am in the prime of senility.
- If you know how to spend less than you get, you have the philosopher's stone.
- If you would be wealthy, think of saving as well as getting.
- If you would know the value of money, go try to borrow some; for he that goes a-borrowing goes a-sorrowing.
- If you would not be forgotten as soon as you are dead and rotten, either write something worth reading or do things worth the writing.
- If you would persuade, you must appeal to interest rather than intellect.
- If you wouldst live long, live well, for folly and wickedness shorten life.
- If your head is wax, don't walk in the sun.
- Never leave that till tomorrow which you can do today.
- Old boys have their playthings as well as young ones; the difference is only in the price.

- Remember not only to say the right thing in the right place, but far more difficult still, to leave unsaid the wrong thing at the tempting moment.
- Search others for their virtues, thyself for thy vices.
- Sloth makes all things difficult, but industry, all things easy. He that rises late must trot all day, and shall scarce overtake his business at night, while laziness travels so slowly that poverty soon overtakes him.
- So convenient a thing it is to be a reasonable creature, since it enables one to find or make a reason for everything one has a mind to do.
- There is no kind of dishonesty into which otherwise good people more easily and frequently fall than that of defrauding the government.
- Three may keep a secret, if two of them are dead.
- Well done is better than well said.
- Who is rich? He that is content. Who is that? Nobody.
- Who is wise? He that learns from every One. Who is powerful? He that governs his Passions. Who is rich? He that is content. Who is that? Nobody.
- You may delay, but time will not.
- Dost thou love life? Then do not squander time, for that's the stuff life is made of.

- Those who would give up essential liberty to purchase a little temporary safety deserve neither liberty nor safety.
- But in this world nothing can be said to be certain, except death and taxes.
- Fish and visitors smell in three days.
- To lengthen thy life, lessen thy meals.
- Wish not so much to live long as to live well.
- Creditors have better memories than debtors.

Freud, Sigmund

- America is a mistake, a giant mistake.
- Everywhere I go I find a poet has been there before me.
- From error to error one discovers the entire truth.
- Men are more moral than they think and far more immoral than they can imagine.
- The goal of all life is death.
- Anatomy is destiny.
- We are certainly getting ahead; if I am Moses, then you are Joshua and will take possession of the promised land of psychiatry, which I shall only be able to glimpse from afar.

- The more the fruits of knowledge become accessible to men, the more widespread is the decline of religious belief.

Fuller, Thomas

- A gift, with a kind countenance, is a double present.
- An ounce of cheerfulness is worth a pound of sadness to serve God with.
- Anger is one of the sinners of the soul.
- Be a friend to thyself, and others will be so too.
- Be not extravagantly high in expression of thy commendations of men thou likest, it may make the hearer's stomach rise.
- Enquire not what boils in another's pot.
- If it were not for hope, the heart would break.
- If thou are a master, be sometimes blind; if a servant, sometimes deaf.
- If we are bound to forgive an enemy, we are not bound to trust him.
- It is madness for sheep to talk peace with a wolf.
- Judge of thine improvement, not by what thou speakest or writest, but by the firmness of thy mind, and the government of thy passions and affections.

- Learning makes a man fit company for himself.
- Many would be cowards if they had courage enough.
- Purchase not friends by gifts; when thou ceasest to give, such will cease to love.
- Some have been thought brave because they were afraid to run away.
- The great end of life is not knowledge, but action.
- Trust thyself only, and another shall not betray thee.
- Know most of the rooms of thy native country before thou goest over the threshold thereof.
- He that is busy is tempted by but one devil; he that is idle, by a legion.

G

Gabor, Zsa Zsa

- I know nothing about sex because I was always married.
- I never hated a man enough to give him his diamonds back.

Galbraith, John Kenneth

- Economics is extremely useful as a form of employment for economists.
- If all else fails, immortality can always be assured by spectacular error.
- It is a far, far better thing to have a firm anchor in nonsense than to put out on the troubled sea of thought.
- Meetings are indispensable when you don't want to do anything.
- Nothing is so admirable in politics as a short memory.

- Politics is not the art of the possible. It consists in choosing between the disastrous and the unpalatable.
- The conventional view serves to protect us from the painful job of thinking.
- The happiest time of anyone's life is just after the first divorce.
- The modern conservative is engaged in one of man's oldest exercises in moral philosophy; that is, the search for a superior moral justification for selfishness.
- The only function of economic forecasting is to make astrology look respectable.
- Under capitalism, man exploits man. Under communism, it's just the opposite.
- Where humor is concerned there are no standards - no one can say what is good or bad, although you can be sure that everyone will.
- You will find that the State is the kind of organization which, though it does big things badly, does small things badly, too.

Gandhi, Indira

- You cannot shake hands with a clenched fist.

- My grandfather once told me that there are two kinds of people: those who work and those who take the credit. He told me to try to be in the first group; there was less competition there.
- My grandfather once told me that there were two kinds of people: those who do the work and those who take the credit. He told me to try to be in the first group; there was much less competition.
- We must learn to be still in the midst of activity and to be vibrantly alive in repose.

Gandhi, Mahatma

- Always aim at complete harmony of thought and word and deed. Always aim at purifying your thoughts and everything will be well.
- As long as you derive inner help and comfort from anything, keep it.
- Freedom is not worth having if it does not include the freedom to make mistakes.
- Happiness is when what you think, what you say, and what you do are in harmony.
- Hate the sin, love the sinner.
- Honest differences are often a healthy sign of progress.

- Honest disagreement is often a good sign of progress.
- I believe in equality for everyone, except reporters and photographers.
- I cannot teach you violence, as I do not myself believe in it. I can only teach you not to bow your heads before any one even at the cost of your life.
- I object to violence because when it appears to do good, the good is only temporary; the evil it does is permanent.
- I want freedom for the full expression of my personality.
- In the attitude of silence the soul finds the path in a clearer light, and what is elusive and deceptive resolves itself into crystal clearness. Our life is a long and arduous quest after Truth.
- Indolence is a delightful but distressing state; we must be doing something to be happy.
- It is better to be violent, if there is violence in our hearts, than to put on the cloak of nonviolence to cover impotence.
- It is unwise to be too sure of one's own wisdom. It is healthy to be reminded that the strongest might weaken and the wisest might err.
- One needs to be slow to form convictions, but once formed they must be defended against the heaviest odds.

- Strength does not come from physical capacity. It comes from an indomitable will.
- The weak can never forgive. Forgiveness is the attribute of the strong.
- Whatever you do will be insignificant, but it is very important that you do it.
- When I despair, I remember that all through history the ways of truth and love have always won. There have been tyrants, and murderers, and for a time they can seem invincible, but in the end they always fall. Think of it—always.
- You must be the change you want to see in the world.
- You must not lose faith in humanity. Humanity is an ocean; if a few drops of the ocean are dirty, the ocean does not become dirty.
- What difference does it make to the dead, the orphans and the homeless, whether the mad destruction is wrought under the name of totalitarianism or the holy name of liberty or democracy?
- Victory attained by violence is tantamount to a defeat, for it is momentary.
- An eye for an eye makes the whole world blind.
- I think it would be a good idea.

- Freedom is not worth having if it does not connote freedom to err. It passes my comprehension how human beings, be they ever so experienced and able, can delight in depriving other human beings of that precious right.

Gay, John

- Cowards are cruel, but the brave Love mercy, and delight to save.
- Fill it up. I take as large draughts of liquor as I did of love. I hate a flincher in either.
- Envy is a kind of praise.
- The luxury of doing good surpasses every other personal enjoyment.

Gibran, Kahlil

- Every man loves two women;the one is the creation of his imagination and the other is not yet born.
- Generosity is giving more than you can, and pride is taking less than you need.
- God made Truth with many doors to welcome every believer who knocks on them.

- I have learnt silence from the talkative, toleration from the intolerant, and kindness from the unkind; yet strange, I am ungrateful to these teachers.
- If indeed you must be candid, be candid beautifully.
- If you cannot work with love but only with distaste, it is better that you should leave your work.
- If you reveal your secrets to the wind you should not blame the wind for revealing them to the trees.
- In the sweetness of friendship; let there be laughter and the sharing of pleasures. For in the dew of little things the heart finds its morning and is refreshed.
- It is well to give when asked, but it is better to give unasked, through understanding.
- Out of suffering have emerged the strongest souls; the most massive characters are seared with scars.
- Say not, 'I have found the truth,' but rather, 'I have found a truth.'
- The deeper sorrow carves into your being the more joy you can contain.
- The lights of stars that were extinguished ages ago still reaches us. So it is with great men who died centuries ago, but still reach us with the radiations of their personalities.

- The optomist sees the rose and not its thorns; the pessimist stares at the thorns, oblivious of the rose.
- To understand the heart and mind of a person, look not at what he has already achieved, but at what he aspires to do.
- Yesterday is but today's memory, tomorrow is today's dream.
- In battling evil, excess is good; for he who is moderate in announcing the truth is presenting half-truth. He conceals the other half out of fear of the people's wrath.
- It is well to give when asked but it is better to give unasked, through understanding.
- Yes, there is a Nirvanah; it is leading your sheep to a green pasture, and in putting your child to sleep, and in writing the last line of your poem.
- And in the sweetness of friendship let there be laughter and the sharing of pleasures. For in the dew of little things the heart finds its morning and is refreshed.

Goethe, Johann Wolfgang von

- A man can stand anything except a succession of ordinary days.

- Against criticism a man can neither protest nor defend himself; he must act in spite of it, and then it will gradually yield to him.
- All truly wise thoughts have been thoughts already thousands of times; but to make them truly ours, we must think them over again honestly, till they take root in our personal experience.
- Anecdotes and maxims are rich treasures to the man of the world, for he knows how to introduce the former at fit place in conversation.
- Beware of dissipating your powers; strive constantly to concentrate them. Genius thinks it can do whatever it sees others doing, but is sure to repent of every ill-judged outlay.
- Divide and rule, a sound motto. Unite and lead, a better one.
- Enjoy when you can, and endure when you must.
- Everything in the world may be endured except continued prosperity.
- How can you come to know yourself? Never by thinking, always by doing. Try to do your duty, and you'll know right away what you amount to.
- If any man wish to write in a clear style, let him be first clear in his thoughts; and if any would write in a noble style, let him first possess a noble soul.

- If children grew up according to early indications, we should have nothing but geniuses.
- Men show their characters in nothing more clearly than in what they think laughable.
- Nothing is worse than active ignorance.
- Nothing is worth more than this day.
- One ought, every day at least, to hear a little song, read a good poem, see a fine picture, and if it were possible, to speak a few reasonable words.
- Science arose from poetry—when times change the two can meet again on a higher level as friends.
- So divinely is the world organized that every one of us, in our place and time, is in balance with everything else.
- That is the true season of love, when we believe that we alone can love, that no one could ever have loved so before us, and that no one will love in the same way after us.
- The intelligent man finds almost everything ridiculous, the sensible man hardly anything.
- There is nothing more dreadful than imagination without taste.
- There is nothing worse than aggressive stupidity.
- To be pleased with one's limits is a wretched state.

- Treat a man as he appears to be, and you make him worse. But treat a man as if he were what he potentially could be, and you make him what he should be.
- We are never deceived; we deceive ourselves.
- We must always change, renew, rejuvenate ourselves; otherwise we harden.
- Whatever you can do or dream, begin it.
- When ideas fail, words come in very handy.
- As soon as you trust yourself, you will know how to live.

Goldman, Emma

- Crime is naught but misdirected energy.
- The strongest bulwark of authority is uniformity; the least divergence from it is the greatest crime.

Goldsmith, Oliver

- Don't let us make imaginary evils, when you know we have so many real ones to encounter.
- Hope, like the gleaming taper's light, Adorns and cheers our way; And still, as darker grows the night, Emits a brighter ray.

- Ill fares the land, to hast'ning ill a prey,
  Where wealth accumulates, and men decay;
  Princes and Lords may flourish, or may fade:
  A breath can make them, as a breath has made;
  but a bold peasantry, their country's pride,
  When once destroyed can never be supplied.

Graves, Robert

- Every English poet should master the rules of grammar before he attempts to bend or break them.
- The remarkable thing about Shakespeare is that he really is very good, in spite of all the people who say he is very good.

Gray, Thomas

- Yet ah! why should they know their fate,
  Since sorrow never comes too late,
  And happiness too swiftly flies?
  Thought would destroy their paradise.
  No more; where ignorance is bliss,
  'Tis folly to be wise.

Greer, Germaine

- Human beings have an inalienable right to invent themselves.
- Probably the only place where a man can feel really secure is in a maximum security prison, except for the imminent threat of release.

H

Hardy, Thomas

- A man's silence is wonderful to listen to.
- Not right out, but stealthily, like a parson's damn.

Hawthorne, Nathaniel

- A bodily disease which we look upon as whole and entire within itself, may, after all, be but a symptom of some ailment in the spiritual part.
- Happiness is as a butterfly which, when pursued, is always beyond our grasp, but which if you will sit down quietly, may alight upon you.
- I cannot endure to waste anything as precious as autumn sunshine by staying in the house. So I spend almost all the daylight hours in the open air.
- No man, for any considerable period, can wear one face to himself and another to the multitude, without finally getting bewildered as to which may be true.

- The world owes all its onward impulses to men ill at ease. The happy man inevitably confines himself within ancient limits.
- What other dungeon is so dark as one's own heart! What jailer so inexorable as one's self!

Hazlitt, William

- He who undervalues himself is justly undervalued by others.
- If you think you can win, you can win. Faith is necessary to victory.
- Man is the only animal that laughs and weeps, for he is the only animal that is struck with the difference between what things are and what they ought to be.
- Men of genius do not excel in any profession because they labor in it, but they labor in it because they excel.
- The love of liberty is the love of others; the love of power is the love of ourselves.
- The way to procure insults is to submit to them: a man meets with no more respect than he exacts.
- When a thing ceases to be a subject of controversy, it ceases to be a subject of interest.

- Without the aid of prejudice and custom I should not be able to find my way across the room.

Hemingway, Ernest

- Always do sober what you said you'd do drunk. That will teach you to keep your mouth shut.
- Happiness in intelligent people is the rarest thing I know.
- I still need more healthy rest in order to work at my best. My health is the main capital I have and I want to administer it intelligently.
- Never confuse movement with action.
- When people talk, listen completely. Most people never listen.
- Certainly there is no hunting like the hunting of man and those who have hunted armed men long enough and liked it, never really care for anything else thereafter.
- Let him think I am more man than I am and I will be so.

Herold, Don

- There's one thing about baldness; it's neat.

- There is nobody so irritating as somebody with less intelligence and more sense than we have.

Hoffer, Eric

- Absolute faith corrupts as absolutely as absolute power.
- Action is at bottom a swinging and flailing of the arms to regain one's balance and keep afloat.
- It is a sign of a creeping inner death when we no longer can praise the living.
- It is thus with most of us; we are what other people say we are. We know ourselves chiefly by hearsay.
- It still hold true that man is most uniquely human when he turns obstacles into opportunities.
- Our greatest pretenses are built up not to hide the evil and the ugly in us, but our emptiness. The hardest thing to hide is something that is not there.
- Power corrupts the few, while weakness corrupts the many.
- Retribution often means that we eventually do to ourselves what we have done unto others.
- Rudeness is the weak man's imitation of strength.
- The opposite of the religious fanatic is not the fanatical atheist but the gentle cynic who cares not whether there is a god or not.

- We are more ready to try the untried when what we do is inconsequential. Hence the fact that many inventions had their birth as toys.
- We are told that talent creates its own opportunities. But it sometimes seems that intense desire creates not only its own opportunities, but its own talents.
- We have perhaps a natural fear of ends. We would rather be always on the way than arrive. Given the means, we hang on to them and often forget the ends.
- We lie the loudest when we lie to ourselves.
- When people are free to do as they please, they usually imitate each other.
- You can discover what your enemy fears most by observing the means he uses to frighten you.
- The poor on the borderline of starvation live purposeful lives. To be engaged in a desperate struggle for food and shelter is to be wholly free from a sense of futility.
- A preoccupation with the future not only prevents us from seeing the present as it is but often prompts us to rearrange the past.
- It is when power is wedded to chronic fear that it becomes formidable.

Hubbard, Elbert

- An ounce of loyalty is worth a pound of cleverness.
- Don't take life too seriously. You'll never get out of it alive.
- Editor: a person employed by a newspaper, whose business it is to separate the wheat from the chaff, and to see that the chaff is printed.
- Enthusiasm is the great hill-climber.
- Folks who never do any more than they are paid for, never get paid more than they do.
- Genius may have its limitations, but stupidity is not thus handicapped.
- Get happiness out of your work or you may never know what happiness is.
- How many a man has thrown up his hands at a time when a little more effort, a little more patience would have achieved success?
- If men could only know each other, they would neither idolize nor hate.
- Life is just one damned thing after another.
- Many a man's reputation would not know his character if they met on the street.

- Never explain—your friends do not need it and your enemies will not believe you anyway.
- No man needs a vacation so much as the man who has just had one.
- One machine can do the work of fifty ordinary men. No machine can do the work of one extraordinary man.
- The greatest mistake you can make in life is to be continually fearing you will make one.
- The recipe for perpetual ignorance is: be satisfied with your opinions and content with your knowledge.
- To avoid criticism do nothing, say nothing, be nothing.

Hubbard, Kin

- A good listener is usually thinking about something else.
- Boys will be boys, and so will a lot of middle-aged men.
- Classical music is the kind we keep thinking will turn into a tune.
- Don't knock the weather. If it didn't change once in a while, nine out of ten people couldn't start a conversation.

- Everything comes to him who waits but a loaned book.
- Honesty pays, but it doesn't seem to pay enough to suit some people.
- It is pretty hard to tell what does bring happiness; poverty and wealth have both failed.
- Men are not punished for their sins, but by them.
- No one can feel as helpless as the owner of a sick goldfish.
- Nothing is as irritating as the fellow who chats pleasantly while he's overcharging you.
- Now and then an innocent man is sent to the legislature.
- So far I haven't heard of anybody who wants to stop living on account of the cost.
- The only way to entertain some folks is to listen to them.
- The safest way to double your money is to fold it over and put it in your pocket.
- There is plenty of peace in any home where the family doesn't make the mistake of trying to get together.
- There's no secret about success. Did you ever know a successful man who didn't tell you about it?

Huxley, Thomas

- Agnosticism simply means that a man shall not say he knows or believes that for which he has no grounds for professing to believe.
- Every great advance in natural knowledge has involved the absolute rejection of authority.
- God give me strength to face a fact though it slay me.
- I have no faith, very little hope, and as much charity as I can afford.
- If a little knowledge is dangerous, where is the man who has so much as to be out of danger.
- Irrationally held truths may be more harmful than reasoned errors.
- Make up your mind to act decidedly and take the consequences. No good is ever done in this world by hesitation.
- Only one absolute certainty is possible to man, namely that at any given moment the feeling which he has exists.
- Sit down before fact as a little child, be prepared to give up every preconceived notion... or you shall learn nothing.

- The deepest sin against the human mind is to believe things without evidence.
- The great tragedy of Science - the slaying of a beautiful hypothesis by an ugly fact.
- The strongest man in the world is the man who stands alone.
- There is no greater mistake than the hasty conclusion that opinions are worthless because they are badly argued.
- Try to learn something about everything and everything about something.

I

Inge, William Ralph

- A nation is a society united by delusions about its ancestry and by common hatred of its neighbors.
- Events in the past may be roughly divided into those which probably never happened and those which do not matter.
- The wise man is he who knows the relative value of things.
- There is no law of progress. Our future is in our own hands, to make or to mar. It will be an uphill fight to the end, and would we have it otherwise? Let no one suppose that evolution will ever exempt us from struggles. 'You forget,' said the Devil, with a chuckle, 'that I have been evolving too.'
- It takes in reality only one to make a quarrel. It is useless for the sheep to pass resolutions in favour of vegetarianism while the wolf remains of a different opinion.

J

James, William

- A great many people think they are thinking when they are really rearranging their prejudices.
- As a rule we disbelieve all the facts and theories for which we have no use.
- Be not afraid of life. Believe that life is worth living, and your belief will help create the fact.
- Human beings, by changing the inner attitudes of their minds, can change the outer aspects of their lives.
- The art of being wise is the art of knowing what to overlook.
- The greatest discovery of my generation is that a human being can alter his life by altering his attitudes of mind.
- The greatest use of life is to spend it for something that will outlast it.
- There is only one thing a philosopher can be relied upon to do, and that is to contradict other philosophers.

- Whenever two people meet, there are really six people present. There is each man as he sees himself, each man as the other person sees him, and each man as he really is.

Johnson, Samuel

- A cucumber should be well-sliced, dressed with pepper and vinegar, and then thrown out.
- A man is very apt to complain of the ingratitude of those who have risen far above him.
- Almost all absurdity of conduct arises from the imitation of those whom we cannot resemble.
- As I know more of mankind I expect less of them, and am ready now to call a man a good man upon easier terms than I was formerly.
- Curiosity is one of the permanent and certain characteristics of a vigorous mind.
- Do not accustom yourself to use big words for little matters.
- Don't think of retiring from the world until the world will be sorry that you retire. I hate a fellow whom pride or cowardice or laziness drives into a corner, and who does nothing when he is there but sit and growl. Let him come out as I do, and bark.

- Every quotation contributes something to the stability or enlargement of the language.
- Few things are impossible to diligence and skill. Great works are performed not by strength, but perseverance.
- Hope is itself a species of happiness, and, perhaps, the chief happiness which this world affords.
- Hope is necessary in every condition.
- If a man does not make new acquaintances as he advances through life, he will soon find himself alone. A man should keep his friendships in constant repair.
- If you are idle, be not solitary; if you are solitary be not idle.
- In order that all men may be taught to speak truth, it is necessary that all likewise should learn to hear it.
- Integrity without knowledge is weak and useless, and knowledge without integrity is dangerous and dreadful.
- It is better to live rich than to die rich.
- It is better to suffer wrong than to do it, and happier to be sometimes cheated than not to trust.
- Love is the wisdom of the fool and the folly of the wise.

- Men have been wise in many different modes; but they have always laughed the same way.
- Of all noises, I think music is the least disagreeable.
- Of all the griefs that harass the distrest, Sure the most bitter is a scornful jest.
- People need to be reminded more often than they need to be instructed.
- Praise, like gold and diamonds, owes its value only to its scarcity.
- Self-confidence is the first requisite to great undertakings.
- Silence propagates itself, and the longer talk has been suspended, the more difficult it is to find anything to say.
- Such seems to be the disposition of man, that whatever makes a distinction produces rivalry.
- The world is not yet exhaused; let me see something tomorrow which I never saw before.
- There are, in every age, new errors to be rectified and new prejudices to be opposed.
- We are inclined to believe those whom we do not know because they have never deceived us.
- What is written without effort is in general read without pleasure.

- While grief is fresh, every attempt to divert only irritates. You must wait till it be digested, and then amusement will dissipate the remains of it.
- Wine makes a man more pleased with himself; I do not say that it makes him more pleasing to others.
- You teach your daughters the diameters of the planets and wonder when you are done that they do not delight in your company.
- A man may be so much of everything that he is nothing of anything.
- Your manuscript is both good and original, but the part that is good is not original and the part that is original is not good.
- The true measure of a man is how he treats someone who can do him absolutely no good.
- Classical quotation is the parole of literary men all over the world.
- It matters not how a man dies, but how he lives. The act of dying is not of importance, it lasts so short a time.
- No man will be a sailor who has contrivance enough to get himself into jail; for being in a ship is being in a jail, with the chance of being drowned.
- Read over your compositions, and wherever you meet with a passage which you think is particularly fine, strike it out.

- Men are generally idle, and ready to satisfy themselves, and intimidate the industry of others, by calling that impossible which is only difficult.
- What we hope ever to do with ease we may learn first to do with diligence.
- Knowledge is of two kinds. We know a subject ourselves, or we know where we can find information on it.
- Mankind have a great aversion to intellectual labor; but even supposing knowledge to be easily attainable, more people would be content to be ignorant than would take even a little trouble to acquire it.
- Patriotism is the last refuge of a scoundrel.

Joyce, James

- Mistakes are the portals of discovery.
- The artist, like the God of creation, remains within or behind or beyond or above his handiwork, invisible, refined out of existence, indifferent, paring his fingernails.

Jung, Carl

- Every form of addiction is bad, no matter whether the narcotic be alcohol, morphine or idealism.
- Everything that irritates us about others can lead us to a better understanding of ourselves.
- Everything that irritates us about others can lead us to an understanding of ourselves.
- Nobody, as long as he moves about among the chaotic currents of life, is without trouble.
- Nothing has a stronger influence psychologically on their environment and especially on their children than the unlived life of the parent.
- The creation of something new is not accomplished by the intellect but by the play instinct acting from inner necessity. The creative mind plays with the objects it loves.
- The healthy man does not torture others - generally it is the tortured who turn into torturers.
- The meeting of two personalities is like the contact of two chemical substances: if there is any reaction, both are transformed.
- The shoe that fits one person pinches another; there is no recipe for living that suits all cases.
- We cannot change anything unless we accept it. Condemnation does not liberate, it oppresses.

- As far as we can discern, the sole purpose of human existence is to kindle a light in the darkness of mere being.
- The least of things with a meaning is worth more in life than the greatest of things without it.
- Where love rules, there is no will to power, and where power predominates, love is lacking. The one is the shadow of the other.

K

Kafka, Franz

- A book must be the ax for the frozen sea within us.
- Anything that has real and lasting value is always a gift from within.
- There art two cardinal sins from which all others spring: Impatience and Laziness.
- Youth is happy because it has the capacity to see beauty. Anyone who keeps the ability to see beauty never grows old.

Keats, John

- I am certain of nothing but the holiness of the heart's affections and the truth of imagination. What the imagination seizes as beauty must be truth - whether it existed before or not.
- I love you the more that I believe you have liked me for my own sake and for nothing else.

- Poetry should please by a fine excess and not by singularity. It should strike the reader as a wording of his own highest thoughts, and appear almost as a remembrance.
- Tis the witching hour of night, Or bed is the moon and bright, And the stars they glisten, glisten, Seeming with bright eyes to listen For what listen they?
- Beauty is truth, truth beauty. That is all ye know, and all ye need to know.

Kennedy, John F.

- Change is the law of life. And those who look only to the past or present are certain to miss the future.
- Forgive your enemies, but never forget their names.
- If we cannot end now our differences, at least we can help make the world safe for diversity.
- Let us think of education as the means of developing our greatest abilities, because in each of us there is a private hope and dream which, fulfilled, can be translated into benefit for everyone and greater strength for our nation.
- Liberty without learning is always in peril; learning without liberty is always in vain.

- Our problems are man-made, therefore they may be solved by man. No problem of human destiny is beyond human beings.

- So, let us not be blind to our differences - but let us also direct attention to our common interests and to the means by which those differences can be resolved.

- The American, by nature, is optimistic. He is experimental, an inventor and a builder who builds best when called upon to build greatly.

- The ancient Greek definition of happiness was the full use of your powers along lines of excellence.

- The great enemy of the truth is very often not the lie — deliberate, contrived and dishonest, but the myth, persistent, persuasive, and unrealistic. Belief in myths allows the comfort of opinion without the discomfort of thought.

- The great French Marshall Lyautey once asked his gardener to plant a tree. The gardener objected that the tree was slow growing and would not reach maturity for 100 years. The Marshall replied, 'In that case, there is no time to lose; plant it this afternoon!'

- The time to repair the roof is when the sun is shining.

- There are risks and costs to a program of action. But they are far less than the long-range risks and costs of comfortable inaction.

- Washington is a city of Southern efficiency and Northern charm.
- We must use time as a tool, not as a crutch.
- We set sail on this new sea because there is knowledge to be gained.
- We stand for freedom. That is our conviction for ourselves; that is our only commitment to others.
- When we got into office, the thing that surprised me the most was that things were as bad as we'd been saying they were.
- Those who make peaceful revolution impossible will make violent revolution inevitable.
- And so, my fellow americans: ask not what your country can do for you - ask what you can do for your country. My fellow citizens of the world: ask not what America will do for you, but what together we can do for the freedom of man.
- If a free society cannot help the many who are poor, it cannot save the few who are rich.
- We must never forget that art is not a form of propaganda; it is a form of truth.
- For in the final analysis, our most basic common link, is that we all inhabit this small planet, we all breathe the same air, we all cherish our children's futures, and we are all mortal.

- Our problems are man-made, therefore they may be solved by man. And man can be as big as he wants. No problem of human destiny is beyond human beings.
- The ignorance of one voter in a democracy impairs the security of all.
- We need men who can dream of things that never were.
- The Chinese use two brush strokes to write the word 'crisis.' One brush stroke stands for danger; the other for opportunity. In a crisis, be aware of the danger - but recognize the opportunity.

Khrushchev, Nikita

- Berlin is the testicle of the West. When I want the West to scream, I squeeze on Berlin.
- Politicians are the same all over. They promise to build a bridge even where there is no river.
- Whether you like it or not, history is on our side. We will bury you.
- I once said, "We will bury you," and I got into trouble with it. Of course we will not bury you with a shovel. Your own working class will bury you.

Kipling, Rudyard

- Gardens are not made by sitting in the shade.
- He wrapped himself in quotations- as a beggar would enfold himself in the purple of Emperors.
- Often and often afterwards, the beloved Aunt would ask me why I had never told anyone how I was being treated. Children tell little more than animals, for what comes to them they accept as eternally established.
- Take everything you like seriously, except yourselves.
- Once there was The People - Terror gave it birth; Once there was The People, and it made a hell of earth! Earth arose and crushed it. Listen, oh, ye slain! Once there was The People - it shall never be again!
- I keep six honest serving-men (They taught me all I knew); Their names are What and Why and When And How and Where and Who.
- Every woman knows all about everything.
- There's no jealousy in the grave.
- Funny how the new things are the old things.

Kissinger, Henry

- Every civilization that has ever existed has ultimately collapsed.
- History knows no resting places and no plateaus.
- Ninety percent of the politicians give the other ten percent a bad reputation.
- Nobody will ever win the Battle of the Sexes. There's just too much fraternizing with the enemy.
- The absence of alternatives clears the mind marvelously.
- The nice thing about being a celebrity is that when you bore people, they think it's their fault.
- The real distinction is between those who adapt their purposes to reality and those who seek to mold reality in the light of their purposes.
- There cannot be a crisis next week. My schedule is already full.
- University politics are vicious precisely because the stakes are so small.
- The illegal we do immediately. The unconstitutional takes a little longer.
- Each success only buys an admission ticket to a more difficult problem.

L

Lawrence, D. H.

- Be still when you have nothing to say; when genuine passion moves you, say what you've got to say, and say it hot.
- For whereas the mind works in possibilities, the intuitions work in actualities, and what you intuitively desire, that is possible to you. Whereas what you mentally or "consciously" desire is nine times out of ten impossible; hitch your wagon to star, or you will just stay where you are.
- How beautiful maleness is, if it finds its right expression.
- It is a fine thing to establish one's own religion in one's heart, not to be dependent on tradition and second-hand ideals. Life will seem to you, later, not a lesser, but a greater thing.

Lincoln, Abraham

- Always bear in mind that your own resolution to succeed is more important than any one thing.
- Better to remain silent and be thought a fool than to speak out and remove all doubt.
- Discourage litigation. Persuade your neighbors to compromise whenever you can. As a peacemaker the lawyer has superior opportunity of being a good man. There will still be business enough.
- Force is all-conquering, but its victories are short-lived.
- He can compress the most words into the smallest ideas of any man I ever met.
- I am a firm believer in the people. If given the truth, they can be depended upon to meet any national crises. The great point is to bring them the real facts.
- I will prepare and some day my chance will come.
- If I were two-faced, would I be wearing this one?
- If this is coffee, please bring me some tea; but if this is tea, please bring me some coffee.
- If you would win a man to your cause, first convince him that you are his sincere friend.
- It has been my experience that folks who have no vices have very few virtues.

- It is difficult to make a man miserable while he feels worthy of himself and claims kindred to the great God who made him.
- Most folks are about as happy as they make up their minds to be.
- Nearly all men can stand adversity, but if you want to test a man's character, give him power.
- No man has a good enough memory to make a successful liar.
- No man is good enough to govern another man without that other's consent.
- Tact is the ability to describe others as they see themselves.
- That some should be rich, shows that others may become rich, and, hence, is just encouragement to industry and enterprise.
- The probability that we may fail in the struggle ought not to deter us from the support of a cause we believe to be just.
- Whatever you are, be a good one.
- When you have got an elephant by the hind leg, and he is trying to run away, it's best to let him run.
- Whenever I hear anyone arguing for slavery, I feel a strong impulse to see it tried on him personally.

- You cannot escape the responsibility of tomorrow by evading it today.
- You may deceive all the people part of the time, and part of the people all the time, but not all the people all the time.
- 'Tis better to be silent and be thought a fool, than to speak and remove all doubt.
- When I do good, I feel good; when I do bad, I feel bad, and that is my religion.
- You can fool some of the people all of the time, and all of the people some of the time, but you can not fool all of the people all of the time.
- People who like this sort of thing will find this the sort of thing they like.
- Quarrel not at all. No man resolved to make the most of himself can spare time for personal contention.
- Truth is generally the best vindication against slander.
- Character is like a tree and reputation like its shadow. The shadow is what we think of it; the tree is the real thing.
- I have always found that mercy bears richer fruits than strict justice.
- It is for us the living, rather, to be dedicated here to the unfinished work which they who fought here have thus far so nobly advanced.

Longfellow, Henry Wadsworth

- A torn jacket is soon mended; but hard words bruise the heart of a child.
- Age is opportunity no less Than youth itself, though in another dress, And as the evening twilight fades away The sky is filled with stars, invisible by day.
- All things must change to something new, to something strange.
- Give what you have. To someone, it may be better than you dare to think.
- He that respects himself is safe from others. He wears a coat of mail that none can pierce.
- If we could read the secret history of our enemies, we should find in each man's life sorrow and suffering enough to disarm all hostility.
- It is curious to note the old sea-margins of human thought. Each subsiding century reveals some new mystery; we build where monsters used to hide themselves.
- Joy, temperance, and repose, Slam the door on the doctor's nose.
- Learn to labour and to wait.

- Let us, then be up and doing, With a heart for any fate; Still achieving, still pursuing, Learn to labour and to wait.
- Look not mournfully into the past. It comes not back again. Wisely improve the present. It is thine. Go forth to meet the shadowy future, without fear.
- Perseverance is a great element of success. If you only knock long enough and loud enough at the gate, you are sure to wake up somebody.
- Talk not of wasted affection, affection never was wasted, If it enrich not the heart of another, its waters returning Back to their springs, like the rain shall fill them full of refreshment;That which the fountain sends forth returns again to the fountain.
- The heights by great men reached and kept were not attained by sudden flight, but they while their companions slept, were toiling upward in the night.
- We judge ourselves by what we feel capable of doing, while others judge us by what we have already done.
- The love of learning, the sequestered nooks, And all the sweet serenity of books.
- Most people would succeed in small things if they were not troubled with great ambitions.
- To say the least, a town life makes one more tolerant and liberal in one's judgement of others.

Lowell, James Russell

- A poet must need be before his own age, to be even with posterity.
- All the beautiful sentiments in the world weigh less than a single lovely action.
- Creativity is not the finding of a thing, but the making something out of it after it is found.
- Democracy gives every man the right to be his own oppressor.
- Folks never understand the folks they hate.
- In creating, the only hard thing is to begin: a grass blade's no easier to make than an oak.
- Mishaps are like knives, that either serve us or cut us, as we grasp them by the blade or the handle.
- Sincerity is impossible, unless it pervades the whole being, and the pretence of it saps the very foundation of character.
- There is no good arguing with the inevitible. The only argument available with an east wind is to put on your overcoat.
- They are slaves who fear to speak, For the fallen and the weak.

- Toward no crime have men shown themselves so cold-bloodedly cruel as in punishing differences of belief.

- Truth, after all, wears a different face to everybody, and it would be too tedious to wait till all were agreed.

- Whatever you may be sure of, be sure of this, that you are dreadfully like other people.

M

Macaulay, Thomas Babington

- It is possible to be below flattery as well as above it.
- She (the Catholic Church) thoroughly understands what no other Church has ever understood, how to deal with enthusiasts.

Macmillan, Harold

- I have never found, in a long experience of politics, that criticism is ever inhibited by ignorance.
- The wind of change is blowing through the continent. Whether we like it or not, this growth of national consciousness is a political fact.

N

Nathan, George Jean

- I drink to make other people seem more interesting.
- Patriotism is often an arbitrary veneration of real estate above principles.

Nehru, Jawaharlal

- Facts are facts and will not disappear on account of your likes.
- Life is like a game of cards. The hand that is dealt you is determinism; the way you play it is free will.
- Peace is not a relationship of nations. It is a condition of mind brought about by a serenity of soul. Peace is not merely the absence of war. It is also a state of mind. Lasting peace can come only to peaceful people.
- The only alternative to coexistence is codestruction.
- The policy of being too cautious is the greatest risk of all.

- There is no end to the adventures that we can have if only we seek them with our eyes open.

Newman, John Henry Cardinal

- Fear not that thy life shall come to an end, but rather fear that it shall never have a beginning.
- Let us take things as we find them: let us not attempt to distort them into what they are not. We cannot make facts. All our wishing cannot change them. We must use them.

Nietzsche, Friedrich

- A casual stroll through the lunatic asylum shows that faith does not prove anything.
- At times one remains faithful to a cause only because its opponents do not cease to be insipid.
- In heaven all the interesting people are missing.
- In truth, there was only one Christian, and he died on the cross.
- Insanity in individuals is something rare - but in groups, parties, nations and epochs, it is the rule.
- It is hard enough to remember my opinions, without also remembering my reasons for them!

- No price is too high to pay for the privilege of owning yourself.
- One must have a good memory to be able to keep the promises one makes.
- Talking much about oneself can also be a means to conceal oneself.
- The advantage of a bad memory is that one enjoys several times the same good things for the first time.
- The irrationality of a thing is no argument against its existence, rather a condition of it.
- The overman...Who has organized the chaos of his passions, given style to his character, and become creative. Aware of life's terrors, he affirms life without resentment.
- The visionary lies to himself, the liar only to others.
- To forget one's purpose is the commonest form of stupidity.
- To predict the behavior of ordinary people in advance, you only have to assume that they will always try to escape a disagreeable situation with the smallest possible expenditure of intelligence.
- What else is love but understanding and rejoicing in the fact that another person lives, acts, and experiences otherwise than we do…?

- When one has much to put into them, a day has a hundred pockets.
- You need chaos in your soul to give birth to a dancing star.
- There is always some madness in love. But there is also always some reason in madness.
- But thus do I counsel you, my friends: distrust all in whom the impulse to punish is powerful!
- Digressions, objections, delight in mockery, carefree mistrust are signs of health; everything unconditional belongs in pathology.
- Poets are shameless with their experiences: they exploit them.
- He who fights with monsters might take care lest he thereby become a monster. And if you gaze for long into an abyss, the abyss gazes also into you.
- What is done out of love always takes place beyond good and evil.
- Only sick music makes money today.
- The man of knowledge must be able not only to love his enemies but also to hate his friends.
- In Christianity neither morality nor religion come into contact with reality at any point.
- Christianity is called the religion of pity.

- What is good? All that heightens the feeling of power in man, the will to power, power itself. What is bad? All that is born of weakness. What is happiness? The feeling that power is growing, that resistance is overcome.

Nixon, Richard M.

- Sure there are dishonest men in local government. But there are dishonest men in national government too.
- Always remember others may hate you but those who hate you don't win unless you hate them. And then you destroy yourself.

O

Orwell, George

- Every generation imagines itself to be more intelligent than the one that went before it, and wiser than the one that comes after it.
- In a time of universal deceit, telling the truth is a revolutionary act.
- On the whole human beings want to be good, but not too good, and not quite all the time.
- To see what is in front of one's nose needs a constant struggle.
- It was a bright cold day in April, and the clocks were striking thirteen.
- All animals are equal but some animals are more equal than others.
- In certain kinds of writing, particularly in art criticism and literary criticism, it is normal to come across long passages which are almost completely lacking in meaning.
- The quickest way of ending a war is to lose it.

- Political language — and with variations this is true of all political parties, from Conservatives to Anarchists — is designed to make lies sound truthful and murder respectable, and to give an appearance of solidity to pure wind.
- People sleep peaceably in their beds at night only because rough men stand ready to do violence on their behalf. If both the past and the external world exist only in the mind, and if the mind itself is controllable – what then?
- War is a way of shattering to pieces, or pouring into the stratosphere, or sinking in the depths of the sea, materials which might otherwise be used to make the masses too comfortable, and hence, in the long run, too intelligent.

P

Paine, Thomas

- Better fare hard with good men than feast it with bad.
- He that would make his own liberty secure, must guard even his enemy from oppression; for if he violates this duty, he establishes a precedent that will reach to himself.
- Society is produced by our wants and government by our wickedness.
- Such is the irresistible nature of truth that all it asks, and all it wants, is the liberty of appearing.
- The real man smiles in trouble, gathers strength from distress, and grows brave by reflection.
- The world is my country, all mankind are my brethren, and to do good is my religion.
- To argue with a person who has renounced the use of reason is like administering medicine to the dead.

- What we obtain too cheap, we esteem too lightly.
- When we are planning for posterity, we ought to remember that virtue is not hereditary.
- A thing moderately good is not so good as it ought to be. Moderation in temper is always a virtue, but moderation in principle is always a vice.
- When my country, into which I had just set my foot, was set on fire about my ears, it was time to stir. It was time for every man to stir.

Parker, Dorothy

- A little bad taste is like a nice dash of paprika.
- Brevity is the soul of lingerie.
- I don't care what is written about me so long as it isn't true.
- I might repeat to myself slowly and soothingly, a list of quotations beautiful from minds profound - if I can remember any of the damn things.
- I've never been a millionaire but I just know I'd be darling at it.
- If all the girls who attended the Yale prom were laid end to end, I wouldn't be a bit surprised.
- She runs the gamut of emotions from A to B.

- If wild my breast and sore my pride, I bask in dreams of suicide, If cool my heart and high my head I think "How lucky are the dead.
- If you want to know what God thinks of money, just look at the people he gave it to.
- Take care of the luxuries and the necessities will take care of themselves.
- The best way to keep children home is to make the home atmosphere pleasant—and let the air out of the tires.
- This is not a novel to be tossed aside lightly. It should be thrown with great force.
- That would be a good thing for them to cut on my tombstone: Wherever she went, including here, it was against her better judgment.
- They sicken of the calm, who knew the storm.
- The cure for boredom is curiosity. There is no cure for curiosity.
- Oh, life is a glorious cycle of song, A medley of extemporanea; And love is a thing that can never go wrong; And I am Marie of Romania.
- Men seldom make passes At girls who wear glasses.

Proverb, Indian

- Call on God, but row away from the rocks.
- An arch never sleeps.
- Keep five yards from a carriage, ten yards from a horse, and a hundred yards from an elephant; but the distance one should keep from a wicked man cannot be measured.

R

Rowland, Helen

- One man's folly is another man's wife.
- The follies which a man regrets most, in his life, are those which he didn't commit when he had the opportunity.

Ruskin, John

- Every increased possession loads us with new weariness.
- Say all you have to say in the fewest possible words, or your reader will be sure to skip them; and in the plainest possible words or he will certainly misunderstand them.
- Taste is not only a part and index of morality, it is the only morality. The first, and last, and closest trial question to any living creature is "What do you like?" Tell me what you like, I'll tell you what you are.

- The greatest thing a human soul ever does in this world is to see something and tell what it saw in a plain way. Hundreds of people can talk for one who can think, but thousands can think for one who can see. To see clearly is poetry, prophecy and religion, all in one.
- The highest reward for man's toil is not what he gets for it, but what he becomes by it.
- What we think, or what we know, or what we believe is, in the end, of little consequence. The only consequence is what we do.
- When a man is wrapped up in himself, he makes a pretty small package.
- When love and skill work together, expect a masterpiece.
- You will find that the mere resolve not to be useless, and the honest desire to help other people, will, in the quickest and delicatest ways, improve yourself.
- There is scarcely anything in the world that some man cannot make a little worse, and sell a little more cheaply. The person who buys on price alone is this man's lawful prey.
- We require from buildings two kinds of goodness: first, the doing their practical duty well: then that they be graceful and pleasing in doing it.
- Let us reform our schools, and we shall find little reform needed in our prisons.

- In order that people may be happy in their work, these three things are needed: They must be fit for it. They must not do too much of it. And they must have a sense of success in it.
- Of all the pulpits from which human voice is ever sent forth, there is none from which it reaches so far as from the grave.

Russell, Bertrand

- A stupid man's report of what a clever man says can never be accurate, because he unconsciously translates what he hears into something he can understand.
- All movements go too far.
- Do not fear to be eccentric in opinion, for every opinion now accepted was once eccentric.
- Everything is vague to a degree you do not realize till you have tried to make it precise.
- Government can easily exist without laws, but law cannot exist without government.
- I think we ought always to entertain our opinions with some measure of doubt. I shouldn't wish people dogmatically to believe any philosophy, not even mine.

- I would never die for my beliefs because I might be wrong.
- If there were in the world today any large number of people who desired their own happiness more than they desired the unhappiness of others, we could have paradise in a few years.
- In all affairs it's a healthy thing now and then to hang a question mark on the things you have long taken for granted.
- In the part of this universe that we know there is great injustice, and often the good suffer, and often the wicked prosper, and one hardly knows which of those is the more annoying.
- It has been said that man is a rational animal. All my life I have been searching for evidence which could support this.
- It is a waste of energy to be angry with a man who behaves badly, just as it is to be angry with a car that won't go.
- Life is nothing but a competition to be the criminal rather than the victim.
- Many people would sooner die than think; In fact, they do so.
- Mathematics, rightly viewed, possesses not only truth, but supreme beauty - a beauty cold and austere, like that of sculpture.

- No one gossips about other people's secret virtues.
- Our great democracies still tend to think that a stupid man is more likely to be honest than a clever man.
- Patriotism is the willingness to kill and be killed for trivial reasons.
- Patriots always talk of dying for their country but never of killing for their country.
- Science may set limits to knowledge, but should not set limits to imagination.
- So far as I can remember, there is not one word in the Gospels in praise of intelligence.
- The good life, as I conceive it, is a happy life. I do not mean that if you are good you will be happy - I mean that if you are happy you will be good.
- The greatest challenge to any thinker is stating the problem in a way that will allow a solution.
- The main things which seem to me important on their own account, and not merely as means to other things, are knowledge, art, instinctive happiness, and relations of friendship or affection.
- The most savage controversies are those about matters as to which there is no good evidence either way.

- The people who are regarded as moral luminaries are those who forego ordinary pleasures themselves and find compensation in interfering with the pleasures of others.
- The place of the father in the modern suburban family is a very small one, particularly if he plays golf.
- The time you enjoy wasting is not wasted time.
- The true spirit of delight, the exaltation, the sense of being more than Man, which is the touchstone of the highest excellence, is to be found in mathematics as surely as in poetry.
- The universe may have a purpose, but nothing we know suggests that, if so, this purpose has any similarity to ours.
- The whole problem with the world is that fools and fanatics are always so certain of themselves, but wiser people so full of doubts.
- There are two motives for reading a book: one, that you enjoy it; the other, that you can boast about it.
- There is much pleasure to be gained from useless knowledge.
- There is no nonsense so errant that it cannot be made the creed of the vast majority by adequate governmental action.

- This is one of those views which are so absolutely absurd that only very learned men could possibly adopt them.
- This is patently absurd; but whoever wishes to become a philosopher must learn not to be frightened by absurdities.
- To be without some of the things you want is an indispensable part of happiness. .
- Too little liberty brings stagnation and too much brings chaos.
- War does not determine who is right - only who is left.
- What the world needs is not dogma but an attitude of scientific inquiry combined with a belief that the torture of millions is not desirable, whether inflicted by Stalin or by a Deity imagined in the likeness of the believer.
- Not to be absolutely certain is, I think, one of the essential things in rationality.
- When one admits that nothing is certain one must, I think, also admit that some things are much more nearly certain than others.
- Men who are unhappy, like men who sleep badly, are always proud of the fact.
- A sense of duty is useful in work, but offensive in personal relations. People wish to be liked, not be endured with patient resignation.

- Of all forms of caution, caution in love is perhaps the most fatal to true happiness.
- To be able to fill leisure intelligently is the last product of civilization, and at present very few people have reached this level.
- One of the symptoms of an approaching nervous breakdown is the belief that one's work is terribly important.
- To fear love is to fear life, and those who fear life are already three parts dead.
- Mathematics may be defined as the subject in which we never know what we are talking about, nor whether what we are saying is true.
- Every man, wherever he goes, is encompassed by a cloud of comforting convictions, which move with him like flies on a summer day.
- It is undesirable to believe a proposition when there is no ground whatsoever for supposing it is true.
- It is obvious that 'obscenity' is not a term capable of exact legal definition; in the practice of the Courts, it means 'anything that shocks the magistrate.'

S

Saki

- Addresses are given to us to conceal our whereabouts.
- He is one of those people who would be enormously improved by death.
- He's simply got the instinct for being unhappy highly developed.
- The young have aspirations that never come to pass, the old have reminiscences of what never happened.
- A little inaccuracy sometimes saves tons of explanation.

Santayana, George

- A man is morally free when, in full possession of his living humanity, he judges the world, and judges other men, with uncompromising sincerity.
- A man's feet should be planted in his country, but his eyes should survey the world.

- Advertising is the modern substitute for argument; its function is to make the worse appear the better.
- America is a young country with an old mentality.
- Before he sets out, the traveler must possess fixed interests and facilities to be served by travel.
- Before you contradict an old man, my fair friend, you should endeavor to understand him.
- Character is the basis of happiness and happiness the sanction of character.
- Sanity is a madness put to good use.
- Science is nothing but developed perception, interpreted intent, common sense rounded out and minutely articulated.
- Skepticism, like chastity, should not be relinquished too readily.
- The body is an instrument, the mind its function, the witness and reward of its operation.
- The wisest mind has something yet to learn.
- Those who speak most of progress measure it by quantity and not by quality.
- To be interested in the changing seasons is a happier state of mind than to be hopelessly in love with spring.

- To knock a thing down, especially if it is cocked at an arrogant angle, is a deep delight of the blood.
- Why shouldn't things be largely absurd, futile, and transitory? They are so, and we are so, and they and we go very well together.
- Our character...is an omen of our destiny, and the more integrity we have and keep, the simpler and nobler that destiny is likely to be.
- The young man who has not wept is a savage, and the old man who will not laugh is a fool.
- Happiness is the only sanction of life; where happiness fails, existence remains a mad and lamentable experiment.
- Fanaticism consists in redoubling your effort when you have forgotten your aim.
- An artist is a dreamer consenting to dream of the actual world.
- Music is essentially useless, as life is.
- Music is essentially useless, as life is: but both have an ideal extension which lends utility to its conditions.
- Nothing is really so poor and melancholy as art that is interested in itself and not in its subject.
- The truth is cruel, but it can be loved, and it makes free those who have loved it.

- There is no cure for birth and death save to enjoy the interval.
- Those who cannot remember the past are condemned to repeat it.
- For an idea ever to be fashionable is ominous, since it must afterwards be always old-fashioned.
- Intolerance itself is a form of egoism, and to condemn egoism intolerantly is to share it.

Shakespeare, William

- A wretched soul, bruised with adversity,
  We bid be quiet when we hear it cry;
  But were we burdened with like weight of pain,
  As much or more we should ourselves complain.
- Action is eloquence.
- And since you know you cannot see yourself, so well as by reflection, I, your glass, will modestly discover to yourself, that of yourself which you yet know not of.
- And thus I clothe my naked villainy
  With old odd ends, stol'n forth of holy writ;
  And seem a saint, when most I play the devil.
- Assume a virtue, if you have it not.

- Be great in act, as you have been in thought.
- Blow, blow, thou winter wind Thou art not so unkind, As man's ingratitude.
- Conversation should be pleasant without scurrility, witty without affectation, free without indecency, learned without conceitedness, novel without falsehood.
- For they are yet ear-kissing arguments.
- Free from gross passion or of mirth or anger constant in spirit, not swerving with the blood, garnish'd and deck'd in modest compliment, not working with the eye without the ear, and but in purged judgement trusting neither? Such and so finely bolted didst thou seem.
- Glory is like a circle in the water, Which never ceaseth to enlarge itself, Till by broad spreading it disperses to naught.
- God bless thee; and put meekness in thy mind, love, charity, obedience, and true duty!
- He who has injured thee was either stronger or weaker than thee. If weaker, spare him; if stronger, spare thyself.
- His life was gentle; and the elements So mixed in him, that Nature might stand up, And say to all the world, THIS WAS A MAN!

- How poor are they who have not patience! What wound did ever heal but by degrees.
- How use doth breed a habit in a man.
- I am not bound to please thee with my answers.
- I did never know so full a voice issue from so empty a heart: but the saying is true 'The empty vessel makes the greatest sound'.
- I dote on his very absence.
- I feel within me a peace above all earthly dignities, a still and quiet conscience.
- I hate ingratitude more in a man than lying, vainness, babbling, drunkenness, or any taint of vice whose strong corruptioninhabits our frail blood.
- I must be cruel only to be kind; Thus bad begins, and worse remains behind.
- I pray thee cease thy counsel, Which falls into mine ears as profitless as water in a sieve.
- I pray you bear me henceforth from the noise and rumour of the field, where I may think the remnant of my thoughts in peace, and part of this body and my soul with contemplation and devout desires.
- I wasted time, and now doth time waste me.

- I wish you well and so I take my leave, I Pray you know me when we meet again.
- Ill deeds are doubled with an evil word.
- In a false quarrel there is no true valour.
- In peace there's nothing so becomes a man as modest stillness and humility.
- In time we hate that which we often fear.
- When we are born, we cry, that we are come To this great stage of fools.
- While thou livest keep a good tongue in thy head.
- You cram these words into mine ears against the stomach of my sense.
- Your face is a book, where men may read strange matters.
- For aught that I could ever read, Could ever hear by tale or history, The course of true love never did run smooth.
- Lord, what fools these mortals be!
- Love all, trust a few. Do wrong to none.
- No legacy is so rich as honesty.
- Praising what is lost Makes the remembrance dear.
- My salad days,When I was green in judgment.

- Age cannot wither her, nor custom stale Her infinite variety.
- Small to greater matters must give way.
- Since Cleopatra died, I have liv'd in such dishonour that the gods Detest my baseness.
- I have Immortal longings in me.
- Hereafter, in a better world than this, I shall desire more love and knowledge of you.
- The little foolery that wise men have makes a great show.
- I met a fool i' the forest, A motley fool.
- True is it that we have seen better days.
- All the world's a stage, And all the men and women merely players. They have their exits and their entrances; And one man in his time plays many parts...
- The fool doth think he is wise, but the wise man knows himself to be a fool.
- No, 'tis slander, Whose edge is sharper than the sword, whose tongue Outvenoms all the worms of Nile, whose breath Rides on the posting winds, and doth belie All corners of the world.
- A little more than kin, and less than kind.
- Frailty, thy name is woman!

- He was a man, take him for all in all, I shall not look upon his like again.
- But to my mind, though I am native here
And to the manner born, it is a custom
More honoured in the breach than the observance.
- Something is rotten in the state of Denmark.

Shaw, George Bernard

- A day's work is a day's work, neither more nor less, and the man who does it needs a day's sustenance, a night's repose and due leisure, whether he be painter or ploughman.
- A fashion is nothing but an induced epidemic.
- A fool's brain digests philosophy into folly, science into superstition, and art into pedantry. Hence University education.
- A life spent making mistakes is not only more honorable, but more useful than a life spent doing nothing.
- A lifetime of happiness! No man alive could bear it; it would be hell on earth.
- Americans adore me and will go on adoring me until I say something nice about them.

- An American has no sense of privacy. He does not know what it means. There is no such thing in the country.
- Criminals do not die by the hands of the law. They die by the hands of other men.
- Democracy is a device that ensures we shall be governed no better than we deserve.
- England and America are two countries separated by a common language.
- Everything happens to everybody sooner or later if there is time enough.
- Few people think more than two or three times a year; I have made an international reputation for myself by thinking once or twice a week.
- Gambling promises the poor what property performs for the rich—something for nothing.
- Hegel was right when he said that we learn from history that man can never learn anything from history.
- Hell is full of musical amateurs.
- I can forgive Alfred Nobel for having invented dynamite, but only a fiend in human form could have invented the Nobel Prize.
- I often quote myself. It adds spice to my conversation.

- If all economists were laid end to end, they would not reach a conclusion.
- If history repeats itself, and the unexpected always happens, how incapable must Man be of learning from experience.
- If the lesser mind could measure the greater as a footrule can measure a pyramid, there would be finality in universal suffrage. As it is, the political problem remains unsolved.
- If you cannot get rid of the family skeleton, you may as well make it dance.
- Imagination is the beginning of creation. You imagine what you desire, you will what you imagine and at last you create what you will.
- Lack of money is the root of all evil.
- Life does not cease to be funny when people die any more than it ceases to be serious when people laugh.
- Martyrdom is the only way in which a man can become famous without ability.
- Patriotism is your conviction that this country is superior to all other countries because you were born in it.
- Reading made Don Quixote a gentleman. Believing what he read made him mad.

- Self-sacrifice enables us to sacrifice other people without blushing.
- Take the utmost trouble to find the right thing to say, and then say it with the utmost levity.
- The fact that a believer is happier than a skeptic is no more to the point than the fact that a drunken man is happier than a sober one.

Shelley, Percy Bysshe

- If winter comes, can spring be far behind?
- Poetry is the record of the best and happiest moments of the happiest and best minds.
- Théré is a harmony In autumn, and a lustre in its sky, Which through the summer is not heard or seen, As if it could not be, as if it had not been!

Sheridan, Richard Brinsley

- He is indebted to his memory for his jests and to his imagination for his facts.
- Humanity is composed but of two categories, the invalids and the nurses.
- When you meet your antagonist, do everything in a mild and agreeable manner. Let your courage be as keen, but at the same time as polished, as your sword.

Sidney, Sir Philip

- All is but lip-wisdom which wants experience.
- No sword bites so fiercly as an evil tongue.
- They are never alone that are accompanied with noble thoughts.

Smith, Logan Pearsall

- Don't laugh at a youth for his affectations; he is only trying on one face after another to find his own.
- I cannot forgive my friends for dying; I do not find these vanishing acts of theirs at all amusing.
- The denunciation of the young is a necessary part of the hygiene of older people, and greatly assists in the circulation of their blood.
- What music is more enchanting than the voices of young people, when you can't hear what they say?
- The test of a vocation is the love of the drudgery it involves.
- It is the wretchedness of being rich that you have to live with rich people.

- To suppose, as we all suppose, that we could be rich and not behave as the rich behave, is like supposing that we could drink all day and keep absolutely sober.
- How many of our daydreams would darken into nightmares if there seemed any danger of their coming true!
- There are few sorrows, however poignant, in which a good income is of no avail.
- There are two things to aim at in life: first, to get what you want; and, after that, to enjoy it. Only the wisest of mankind achieve the second.
- People say that life is the thing, but I prefer reading.
- All Reformers, however strict their social conscience, live in houses just as big as they can pay for.
- Most people sell their souls, and live with a good conscience on the proceeds.
- When they come downstairs from their Ivory Towers, Idealists are very apt to walk straight into the gutter.

Smith, Sydney

- Errors to be dangerous must have a great deal of truth mingled with them. It is only from this alliance that they can ever obtain an extensive circulation.

- Have the courage to be ignorant of a great number of things, in order to avoid the calamity of being ignorant of everything.
- Live always in the best company when you read.
- Never try to reason the prejudice out of a man. It was not reasoned into him, and cannot be reasoned out.
- There is one piece of advice, in a life of study, which I think no one will object to; and that is, every now and then to be completely idle - to do nothing at all.
- To do anything in this world worth doing, we must not stand back shivering and thinking of the cold and danger, but jump in, and scramble through as well as we can.
- Whatever you are by nature, keep to it; never desert your line of talent. Be what nature intended you for and you will succeed.
- You must not think me necessarily foolish because I am facetious, nor will I consider you necessarily wise because you are grave.
- He had occasional flashes of silence, that made his conversation perfectly delightful.

Steele, Sir Richard

- Reading is to the mind what exercise is to the body.
- Whenever you commend, add your reasons for doing so; it is this which distinguishes the approbation of a man of sense from the flattery of sycophants and admiration of fools.

Stevenson, Robert Louis

- A friend is a gift you give yourself.
- If your morals make you dreary, depend on it , they are wrong.
- It is not much for its beauty that makes a claim upon men's hearts, as for that subtle something, that quality of air that emanates from old trees, that so wonderfully changes and renews a weary spirit.
- It is perhaps a more fortunate destiny to have a taste for collecting shells than to be born a millionaire.
- Keep your fears to yourself, but share your courage with others.
- Perpetual devotion to what a man calls his business, is only to be sustained by perpetual neglect of many other things.

- Politics is perhaps the only profession for which no preparation is thought necessary.
- The cruelest lies are often told in silence.
- The most beautiful adventures are not those we go to seek.
- There is no duty we so much underrate as the duty of being happy.
- To know what you prefer instead of humbly saying Amen to what the world tells you you ought to prefer, is to have kept your soul alive.
- To travel hopefully is a better thing than to arrive.
- You cannot run away from a weakness; you must sometimes fight it out or perish. And if that be so, why not now, and where you stand?

Swift, Jonathan

- A wise man should have money in his head, but not in his heart.
- He was a bold man that first ate an oyster.
- I row after health like a waterman...
- I wonder what fool it was that first invented kissing.
- May you live all the days of your life.

- It is impossible that anything so natural, so necessary, and so universal as death, should ever have been designed by Providence as an evil to mankind.
- It is useless to attempt to reason a man out of a thing he was never reasoned into.
- No wise man ever wished to be younger.
- One of the best rules in conversation is, never to say a thing which any of the company can reasonably wish had been left unsaid.
- Ambition often puts men upon doing the meanest offices; so climbing is performed in the same posture with creeping.
- When a true genius appears in this world, you may know him by this sign, that the dunces are all in confederacy against him.

T

Tennyson, Alfred Lord

- Cast all your cares on God; that anchor holds.
- Hope smiles on the threshold of the year to come, whispering that it will be happier.
- Knowledge comes, but wisdom lingers.
- The greater man the greater courtesy.
- The happiness of a man in this life does not consist in the absence but in the mastery of his passions.
- Tis better to have loved and lost Than never to have loved at all.

Thackeray, William Makepeace

- Attacking is the only secret. Dare and the world always yields; or if it beats you sometimes, dare it again and it will succumb.
- Bravery never goes out of fashion.

Thatcher, Margaret

- Europe was created by history. America was created by philosophy.
- Europe will never be like America. Europe is a product of history. America is a product of philosophy.
- I usually make up my mind about a man in ten seconds; and I very rarely change it.
- If it is once again one against forty-eight, then I am very sorry for the forty-eight.
- I am extraordinarily patient, provided I get my own way in the end.
- To wear your heart on your sleeve isn't a very good plan; you should wear it inside, where it functions best.

Thomas, Dylan

- After thirty nine years this is all I've done.
- I just drank eighteen whiskies. That must be a record.
- Do not go gentle into that good night, Old age should burn and rave at close of day; Rage, rage against the dying of the light.

- An alcoholic is someone you don't like who drinks as much as you do.
- Someone's boring me. I think it's me.

Thoreau, Henry David

- A man is rich in proportion to the number of things he can afford to let alone.
- Any fool can make a rule, and any fool will mind it.
- As if you could kill time without injuring eternity.
- Be true to your work, your word, and your friend.
- Cultivate the habit of early rising. It is unwise to keep the head long on a level with the feet.
- Do not be too moral. You may cheat yourself out of much life. Aim above morality. Be not simply good; be good for something.
- Do not hire a man who does your work for money, but him who does it for love of it.
- Every man is the builder of a temple called his body.
- Go confidently in the direction of your dreams! Live the life you've imagined. As you simplify your life, the laws of the universe will be simpler.

- He enjoys true leisure who has time to improve his soul's estate.
- How vain it is to sit down to write when you have not stood up to live.
- I know of no more encouraging fact than the unquestioned ability of a man to elevate his life by conscious endeavor.
- I once had a sparrow alight upon my shoulder for a moment, while I was hoeing in a village garden, and I felt that I was more distinguished by that circumstance that I should have been by any epaulet I could have worn.
- If you have built castles in the air, your work need not be lost; that is where they should be. Now put the foundations under them.
- If you would convince a man that he does wrong, do right. But do not care to convince him. Men will believe what they see. Let them see.
- If you would convince a man that he does wrong, do right. Men will believe what they see.
- In what concerns you much, do not think that you have companions: know that you are alone in the world.
- In wildness is the preservation of the world.
- It is as hard to see one's self as to look backwards without turning around.

- It is never too late to give up your prejudices.
- Live each season as it passes; breathe the air, drink the drink, taste the fruit, and resign yourself to the influences of each.
- Men are born to succeed, not fail.
- Men have become the tools of their tools.
- Most are engaged in business the greater part of their lives, because the soul abhors a vacuum and they have not discovered any continuous employment for man's nobler faculties.
- My friend is one... who take me for what I am.
- Our life is frittered away by detail. Simplify, simplify.
- Public opinion is a weak tyrant compared with our own private opinion. What a man thinks of himself, that is which determines, or rather indicates, his fate.

Tolstoy, Leo

- Everyone thinks of changing the world, but no one thinks of changing himself.
- Everything that I understand, I understand only because I love.

- Historians are like deaf people who go on answering questions that no one has asked them.
- If one has no vanity in this life of ours, there is no sufficient reason for living.
- In the name of God, stop a moment, cease your work, look around you.
- Happy families are all alike; every unhappy family is unhappy in its own way.

Twain, Mark

- A banker is a fellow who lends you his umbrella when the sun is shining, but wants it back the minute it begins to rain.
- A man cannot be comfortable without his own approval.
- Always acknowledge a fault. This will throw those in authority off their guard and give you an opportunity to commit more.
- Always do right. This will gratify some people and astonish the rest.
- An Englishman is a person who does things because they have been done before. An American is a person who does things because they haven't been done before.

- Barring that natural expression of villainy which we all have, the man looked honest enough.
- Be careful about reading health books. You may die of a misprint.
- By trying we can easily learn to endure adversity — another man's I mean.
- Clothes make the man. Naked people have little or no influence on society.
- Courage is resistance to fear, mastery of fear - not absence of fear.
- Do something every day that you don't want to do; this is the golden rule for acquiring the habit of doing your duty without pain.
- Don't go around saying the world owes you a living. The world owes you nothing. It was here first.
- Don't part with your illusions. When they are gone you may still exist, but you have ceased to live.
- Education: that which reveals to the wise, and conceals from the stupid, the vast limits of their knowledge.
- Facts are stubborn things, but statistics are more pliable.
- Fiction is obliged to stick to possibilities. Truth isn't.

- Get your facts first, and then you can distort them as much as you please.
- Grief can take care of itself, but to get the full value of a joy you must have somebody to divide it with.
- Humor is the great thing, the saving thing. The minute it crops up, all our irritations and resentments slip away and a sunny spirit takes their place.
- I am opposed to millionaires, but it would be dangerous to offer me the position.
- I didn't attend the funeral, but I sent a nice letter saying that I approved of it.
- I don't give a damn for a man that can only spell a word one way.
- I have a higher and grander standard of principle than George Washington. He could not lie; I can, but I won't.
- I have been through some terrible things in my life, some of which actually happened.
- I have never let my schooling interfere with my education.
- I have never taken any exercise except sleeping and resting.
- I thoroughly disapprove of duels. If a man should challenge me, I would take him kindly and forgivingly by the hand and lead him to a quiet place and kill him.

- I was gratified to be able to answer promptly. I said I don't know.
- If you pick up a starving dog and make him prosperous, he will not bite you. This is the principal difference between a dog and a man.
- If you tell the truth you don't have to remember anything.
- In Paris they simply stared when I spoke to them in French; I never did succeed in making those idiots understand their language.
- In religion and politics, people's beliefs and convictions are in almost every case gotten at second hand, and without examination.
- In the first place, God made idiots. That was for practice. Then he made school boards.
- It could probably be shown by facts and figures that there is no distinctly American criminal class except Congress.
- It is better to deserve honors and not have them than to have them and not to deserve them.
- It is better to keep your mouth closed and let people think you are a fool than to open it and remove all doubt.
- It is curious that physical courage should be so common in the world and moral courage so rare.

- It is easier to stay out than get out.
- It usually takes more than three weeks to prepare a good impromptu speech.
- It was wonderful to find America, but it would have been more wonderful to miss it.
- Just the omission of Jane Austen's books alone would make a fairly good library out of a library that hadn't a book in it.
- Keep away from people who try to belittle your ambitions. Small people always do that, but the really great make you feel that you, too, can become great.
- Let us be thankful for the fools. But for them the rest of us could not succeed.
- Let us so live that when we come to die even the undertaker will be sorry.
- Most people are bothered by those passages of Scripture they do not understand, but the passages that bother me are those I do understand.
- My mother had a great deal of trouble with me, but I think she enjoyed it.
- Never put off until tomorrow what you can do the day after tomorrow.
- Often it does seem a pity that Noah and his party did not miss the boat.

- Part of the secret of success in life is to eat what you like and let the food fight it out inside.
- Suppose you were an idiot and suppose you were a member of Congress. But I repeat myself.
- The best way to cheer yourself is to try to cheer someone else up.
- The coldest winter I ever spent was a summer in San Francisco.
- The difference between the right word and the almost right word is the difference between lightning and a lightning bug.
- The human race has one really effective weapon, and that is laughter.
- The man who doesn't read good books has no advantage over the man who can't read them.
- The right word may be effective, but no word was ever as effective as a rightly timed pause.
- The universal brotherhood of man is our most precious possession.

❖ U ❖

Unamuno, Miguel de

- Use harms and even destroys beauty. The noblest function of an object is to be contemplated.
- The skeptic does not mean him who doubts, but him who investigates or researches, as opposed to him who asserts and thinks that he has found.
- Conscience is a sickness.
- Faith which does not doubt is dead faith.
- To fall into a habit is to begin to cease to be.
- Love kills happiness, happiness kills love.

V

Vidal, Gore

- Any American who is prepared to run for president should automatically, by definition, be disqualified from ever doing so.
- Half of the American people have never read a newspaper. Half never voted for President. One hopes it is the same half.
- It is not enough to succeed. Others must fail.
- Never have children, only grandchildren.
- Style is knowing who you are, what you want to say and not giving a damn.
- There is no human problem which could not be solved if people would simply do as I advise.
- Today's public figures can no longer write their own speeches or books, and there is some evidence that they can't read them either.

Voltaire

- A witty saying proves nothing.

- All sects are different, because they come from men; morality is everywhere the same, because it comes from God.
- Anything too stupid to be said is sung.
- Appreciation is a wonderful thing: It makes what is excellent in others belong to us as well.
- Doubt is not a pleasant condition, but certainty is absurd.
- Every man is guilty of all the good he didn't do.
- God is a circle whose center is everywhere and circumference nowhere.
- God is a comedian playing to an audience too afraid to laugh.
- God is always on the side of the big battalions.
- History is a pack of lies we play on the dead.
- I have never made but one prayer to God, a very short one: 'O Lord, make my enemies ridiculous.' And God granted it.
- If God did not exist, it would be necessary to invent him.
- Indeed, history is nothing more than a tableau of crimes and misfortunes.
- Indolence is sweet, and its consequences bitter.
- It is dangerous to be right when the government is wrong.

- It is forbidden to kill; therefore all murderers are punished unless they kill in large numbers and to the sound of trumpets.
- Judge of a man by his questions rather than by his answers.
- Love is a canvas furnished by Nature and embroidered by imagination.
- Love truth, and pardon error.
- Marriage is the only adventure open to the cowardly.
- Men are equal; it is not birth but virtue that makes the difference.
- Prejudice is opinion without judgement.
- Regimen is superior to medicine.
- The art of medicine consists in amusing the patient while nature cures the disease.
- The multitude of books is making us ignorant.
- The secret of being boring is to say everything.
- There is a wide difference between speaking to deceive, and being silent to be impenetrable.
- Those who can make you believe absurdities can make you commit atrocities.

W

Walpole, Horace

- The whole secret of life is to be interested in one thing profoundly and in a thousand things well.
- The world is a tragedy to those who feel, but a comedy to those who think.

Ward, Artemus

- I have given two cousins to war and I stand ready to sacrifice my wife's brother.
- Why is this thus? What is the reason for this thusness?

Washington, George

- Associate yourself with men of good quality if you esteem your own reputation for 'tis better to be alone than in bad company.

- Associate yourself with men of good quality if you esteem your own reputation, for 'tis better to be alone than in bad company.
- Be courteous to all, but intimate with few, and let those few be well tried before you give them your confidence. True friendship is a plant of slow growth, and must undergo and withstand the shocks of adversity before it is entitled to the appellation.
- Be courteous to all, but intimate with few; and let those few be well tried before you give them your confidence.
- Few men have virtue to withstand the highest bidder.
- It's wonderful what we can do if we're always doing.
- Labor to keep alive in your breast that little spark of celestial fire called conscience.
- Our cause is noble; it is the cause of mankind!
- It is better to offer no excuse than a bad one.

Waugh, Evelyn

- It is a curious thing... that every creed promises a paradise which will be absolutely uninhabitable for anyone of civilized taste.

- What is youth except a man or a woman before it is ready or fit to be seen?
- Punctuality is the virtue of the bored.

Webster, John

- There's nothing sooner dry than women's tears.
- We are merely the stars' tennisballs, struck and bandied. Which way please them.

Wells, H. G.

- Adapt or perish, now as ever, is nature's inexorable imperative.
- No passion in the world is equal to the passion to alter someone else's draft.
- We must not allow the clock and the calendar to blind us to the fact that each moment of life is a miracle and mystery.
- The forceps of our minds are clumsy forceps, and crush the truth a little in taking hold of it.
- Human history becomes more and more a race between education and catastrophe.
- Moral indignation is jealousy with a halo.

West, Mae

- He who hesitates is a damned fool.
- His mother should have thrown him away and kept the stork.
- I generally avoid temptation unless I can't resist it.
- Marriage is a great institution, but I'm not ready for an institution yet.
- Too much of a good thing is wonderful.
- You're never too old to become younger.
- Between two evils, I always pick the one I never tried before.

Wilde, Oscar

- A little sincerity is a dangerous thing, and a great deal of it is absolutely fatal.
- A man can be happy with any woman as long as he does not love her.
- Always forgive your enemies; nothing annoys them so much.
- America had often been discovered before Columbus, but it had always been hushed up.

- America is the only country that went from barbarism to decadence without civilization in between.
- Anyone who lives within their means suffers from a lack of imagination.
- Arguments are to be avoided; they are always vulgar and often convincing.
- At twilight, nature is not without loveliness, though perhaps its chief use is to illustrate quotations from the poets.
- iography lends to death a new terror.
- Consistency is the last refuge of the unimaginative.
- Every portrait that is painted with feeling is a portrait of the artist, not of the sitter.
- Fashion is a form of ugliness so intolerable that we have to alter it every six months.
- Genius is born—not paid.
- I always like to know everything about my new friends, and nothing about my old ones.
- I am not young enough to know everything.
- I think that God in creating Man somewhat overestimated his ability.
- I was working on the proof of one of my poems all the morning, and took out a comma. In the afternoon I put it back again.

- If you want to tell people the truth, make them laugh, otherwise they'll kill you.
- Illusion is the first of all pleasures.
- It is a very sad thing that nowadays there is so little useless information.
- It is always a silly thing to give advice, but to give good advice is fatal.
- Man is least himself when he talks in his own person. Give him a mask, and he will tell you the truth.
- Morality, like art, means drawing a line someplace.
- Most modern calendars mar the sweet simplicity of our lives by reminding us that each day that passes is the anniversary of some perfectly uninteresting event.
- Most people are other people. Their thoughts are someone elses opinions, their lives a mimicry, their passions a quotation.
- Music makes one feel so romantic - at least it always gets on one's nerves - which is the same thing nowadays.
- One can survive everything, nowadays, except death, and live down everything except a good reputation.
- One should always play fairly when one has the winning cards.

- Patriotism is the virtue of the vicious.

Woolf, Virginia

- For most of history, Anonymous was a woman.
- If you do not tell the truth about yourself you cannot tell it about other people.
- Literature is strewn with the wreckage of men who have minded beyond reason the opinions of others.
- Women have served all these centuries as looking-glasses possessing the magic and delicious power of reflecting the figure of a man at twice its natural size.
- I meant to write about death, only life came breaking in as usual.
- I have lost friends, some by death... others through sheer inability to cross the street.

Wordsworth, William

- She was a phantom of delight When first she gleam'd upon my sight; A lovely apparition, sent To be a moment's ornament.
- That best portion of a good man's life, His little, nameless, unremembered acts of kindness and of love.

- That best portion of a good man's life, His little, nameless, unremembered acts of kindness and of love.
- The best portion of a good man's life is his little, nameless, unremembered acts of kindness and of love.

Y

Yeats, William Butler

- A pity beyond all telling is hid in the heart of love.
- An aged man is but a paltry thing, a tattered coat upon a stick.
- And say my glory was I had such friends.
- Think like a wise man but communicate in the language of the people.

Young, Edward

- Be wise with speed . A fool at forty is a fool indeed.
- Procrastination is the thief of time.
- Some for renown, on scraps of learning dote, And think they grow immortal as they quote.

Z

Zappa, Frank

- Art is making something out of nothing and selling it.
- Communism doesn't work because people like to own stuff.
- Everybody believes in something and everybody, by virtue of the fact that they believe in something, use that something to support their own existence.
- I think it is good that books still exist, but they do make me sleepy.
- In the fight between you and the world, back the world.
- The United States is a nation of laws: badly written and randomly enforced.
- Without deviation from the norm, progress is not possible.
- Rock journalism is people who can't write interviewing people who can't talk for people who can't read.